Real G's Move in Silence

Lock Down Publications and Ca$h Presents

Real G's Move in Silence

A Novel by *Von Diesel*

Lock Down Publications
Po Box 944
Stockbridge, Ga 30281

Visit our website @
www.lockdownpublications.com

First Edition November 2022
Printed in the United States of America

Lock Down Publications
Like our page on Facebook: Lock Down Publications @
www.facebook.com/lockdownpublications.ldp
Book interior design by: **Shawn Walker**
Edited by: **Sunny Giovanni**

Stay Connected with Us!

Text **LOCKDOWN** to 22828 to stay up-to-date with new releases, sneak peaks, contests and more…
Thank you.

Submission Guideline.

Submit the first three chapters of your completed manuscript to ldpsubmissions@gmail.com, subject line: Your book's title. The manuscript must be in a .doc file and sent as an attachment. Document should be in Times New Roman, double spaced and in size 12 font. Also, provide your synopsis and full contact information. If sending multiple submissions, they must each be in a separate email.

Have a story but no way to send it electronically? You can still submit to LDP/Ca$h Presents. Send in the first three chapters, written or typed, of your completed manuscript to:

LDP: Submissions Dept
Po Box 944
Stockbridge, Ga 30281

DO NOT send original manuscript. Must be a duplicate.

Provide your synopsis and a cover letter containing your full contact information.

Thanks for considering LDP and Ca$h Presents.

PROLOGUE

"No one can stop us now, bro. The competition is no longer a problem, and everybody knows that we run the city," Hit-Man stated, sipping a glass of Hennessey.

Lit sat on the ottoman, puffing on some loud as he thought about all the treacherous things he and his crew had done to take over the cities of Mobile and Birmingham. They had committed murder after murder, until there was no one left standing but them. "Yeah, but where does that leave us now? We lost a lot of good soldiers in the process," he replied.

"Come on, Lit! They knew what they were getting into when they decided to bang with us. It could have easily been one of us lying in the dirt right now. They gave their lives for us, and for that, we will make sure their families are taken care of," Hit-Man spat, walking back and forth across the balcony. "Besides, I know the infamous Antonio is not getting soft on me."

"Nigga, I told you about calling me by my government. I'm not getting soft. I'm just looking at the big picture. Yeah, we control the drug trade, but I want more. I want to open up some businesses to cover up our illegal endeavors," Lit said as the two men looked out at the peaceful city.

"What do you have in mind?"

"I was thinking about investing in a couple of things. Look at what's going on in Biloxi with the casinos. How about we look into that or maybe some apartment complexes?" Lit asked.

"That sounds good and all, but how the hell are we going to get into that when neither one of us has any business experience? We both dropped out of high school and have criminal records."

"I can get Doja to get a business license, so let me worry about that. Let's get out of here and go check on this money. Besides, I have to pick up my kids in a few. I'm taking them to *Jump Air* since I haven't seen them in a month because of all the beef we were in," Lit stated as the two men headed out of the penthouse.

As they stepped off the elevator and headed toward the garage, where their cars were located, they never saw the three black SUVs creeping up on them.

* **

"Damn! What's taking your dad so long to get here? I've called him four times already, and he hasn't even answered once," Shaquana said to little Antonio.

The two of them burst out laughing as they downed their drinks before setting the empty glasses on the table.

Shaquana huffed and then leaned her head back on the couch. "I have to work tonight, so he better hurry up and get here, or you will have to watch the kids for me."

"I have a date tonight, Quana. I told you about that the other day. I've been standing bull up for a minute now. I finally told him that we can chill tonight," Nodie replied.

"He'll be here to get them before your friend comes. Don't act like that," Shaquana stated as she playfully punched her sister in the arm.

Before she could respond, they heard the baby crying in the other room. Shaquana got up and went to get Antonio Jr., and Nodie threw a pillow at her and then grabbed the glasses to refill them.

When Shaquana looked at her son, he was the spitting image of Lit. He couldn't deny him if he tried. She thought back to the day when Lit first came into her parents' pizza shop for a slice. It only took one date for him to win her over. She had never been with a black guy before, so curiosity got the best of her, and once they had sex the first time, she was addicted.

They spent every available moment together that they could. Lit showed her a lot of attention in the beginning, but once he started wreaking havoc from city to city, he stopped being around her so much. He didn't want her to get caught up in the life that he kept a secret from her.

One day she was driving down the street because she wanted to surprise him with a tattoo that she just got, when she heard rapid gunfire. She saw some guy do a flip in the air and land in the middle of the street, right in front of her car. All of a sudden, someone walked up to the guy lying there, and emptied his clip into him, causing his body to jerk.

She couldn't believe her eyes when she saw the man she was in love with standing with the smoking gun. Their eyes met as he ran up to the passenger side of her car. She unlocked the door as Lit jumped in. No words were spoken as she hit the gas, getting him out of there and away from the crime scene. She never even mentioned what she saw that day. Lit realized he had a girl in his corner who was down for whatever, which made him like her even more.

Now they were engaged to get married and had two beautiful children together. Shaquana knew that he would do anything to protect his family, and she would be by his side no matter what.

"Shaquana! Quana!" Nodie yelled, snapping her out of her thoughts.

Shaquana looked up at her sister and smiled. "Don't he look just like his ugly-ass dad, but more handsome?" Shaquana said, with a smile on her face.

"You're stupid, girl! I just talked to my date and told him that I may be running late, so go ahead and get ready for work. I'll watch the kids until he comes," she told her.

She picked up little Antonio and gave him a bunch of kisses on his cheeks, causing him to chuckle. "Thanks, Sis! I owe you big for this one," she stated as she headed for her room to get dressed.

"You sure do, and I will be collecting for it, too," Nodie replied as she took Lil Antonio into the other room with her.

When Shaquana left for work, she tried calling Lit again, but had the same results. It wasn't like him not to answer her calls. She couldn't shake the feeling that something was wrong. If she only knew that the feeling she was having would soon be a reality.

CHAPTER 1

"Yo, I need your shit for the wrap!" Six-Nine yelled out while standing on the top tier.

"I got you, bro. Give me a second," Lit replied, then turned his attention back to the game. "I'ma let you dig your own grave."

"Ten!" D-Strong said, challenging him. He threw his chips into the pile with the other chips, waiting for everyone to call him.

"I'm down!" Hit-Man said, folding his hand.

"Me, too!" Corey followed.

"I'll call you," Lit said as he put in his chips and then showed his hand. "I have a boat! Aces over kings!"

D-Strong smiled and then laid down his cards on the table for everyone to see. "I have quads," he said, showing that he had four tens, which beat Lit's full house. "I was trying to get you to bet more, but you didn't." He added with a smirk.

"Fuck you, nigga!" Lit yelled, knowing that he had just lost. He got up from the table to go grab something out of his room. He wanted D-Strong to say some slick shit so he could beat his ass, but D-Strong didn't.

Six-Nine walked over to Lit's room and knocked on the door.

Lit invited him inside as he grabbed the soups, cheese, and meat out of his drawer. "What else do you need besides this?" he asked, passing him the food.

"That's it! I have everything else. The water is boiling now. You gonna help me make it, or you still playing poker?"

"Yeah, I'm trying to take these white boys' money. D-Strong's winning right now, but I'm up on paper. Corey's crazy ass calls everything. He don't care if he loses or not!" Lit said as he headed back to the game.

As he walked down the steps, Hit-Man came out of his room and said, "Antonio, when you get a second, I need to holla at you for a minute."

"Stop calling me that, Hit-Man." Lit smirked. They both liked calling each other by their government names to make one another mad. "Give me a few minutes so I can finish getting this easy money real quick."

"That's what I want to talk to you about, bro. I'm talking about some real money, not those soups y'all playing for right now," Hit-Man stated matter-of factly.

Lit continued playing poker for about another hour until everyone lost their chips except for him and D-Strong. They counted them up and played for extras. Afterward, he went upstairs to talk with his Islamic brother about business.

"As-salamu 'alaykum," Lit greeted with the words "peace be unto you" in Arabic. "My bad it took me so long, bro."

"Wa alaikum salaam. It's cool. I just got finished making salat, so you need to do the same," Hit-Man said.

"Alhamdulillahi. I will as soon as you tell me what's up!" Lit replied, leaning on the sink.

"Well, you know I'm leaving this week sometime, and I have that number that the bull gave me to contact him when I touch on the work. I wanted to know if you were still trying to link up with him, too, being that you might also be out. Plus, I wanted to know if he's a trustworthy nigga. We only met him in here, and you already know how niggas come to jail and be all they can be."

Lit smiled because he understood where his man was coming from. Muthafuckas came to jail with Bentleys and Mercedes out there but couldn't even make a phone call or buy commissary. "Bull, is cool. I did some homework on him a couple of days ago, and he's really getting a dollar out there. He even did what he said he was going to do and put money on my account. Did you check yours yet?"

"Naw! I was going to check it when I called my mom later on, but I'll check it now," Hit-Man said as the two walked over to the phone.

"Yo, man! Come here real quick!" Lit yelled up to Six-Nine's room.

"Hold on, nigga. I'm chiefing this shit up right now. I'll be down in a few minutes," he hollered out.

Hit-Man hung up the phone and gave Lit the thumbs up, indicating that his money was also on there. "That nigga did what he said he would. So, I guess he's definitely official. Now I hope he really puts us on when we get out so we can get this bread. That brings me back to the question I asked you. Are you down or what?"

"Damn right I'm down! As long as they drop my case when I go to court, I should be out of this bitch!" Lit told his friend. "How much are we gonna get from him?"

"I'm trying to take whatever he gives us. I know between Mobile and Birmingham, we should be able to move a large amount of it."

"I was under the presumption that you were going to chill out until you get out of rehab," Lit questioned.

"My lawyer said that I don't have to go now. I just needed to give them an address so I can get released. I presented it to my PO, and she approved it already," Hit-Man said with a smile on his face. It was just a waiting process now for him.

Lit had met Hit-Man when he came on the block two months ago, and they hit it off instantly. He considered him to be a very close friend. Not only was he a friend, but he was also Lit's brother in faith. They all were. It was Six-Nine who had piqued Lit's interest about the Islamic Religion. Lit was already Muslim, but he had stopped practicing a while ago. Now, he was back on his deen and going strong.The three of them prayed five times a day together and went to jum'ah every Friday. They tried to make taleem as much as possible, but sometimes they wouldn't call it for their block. Other than that, they were very loyal and dedicated to their belief. Each one of them had their Quran and prayer rug so they could pray in the confinement of their respective cells.

Lit was locked up for getting pulled over with a gun in his car. He was on his way home from seeing some girl in Rosa Parks, when he ran a stop sign. He didn't see the cop parked in the lot across the street. He tried to hide the gun under the seat, but due to him not having a license, it gave them probable cause to search the vehicle. Next thing he knew, he was in Fulton County Jail.

Hit-Man was in the house with his girlfriend, counting perks when his PO unexpectedly showed up. He tried to hide the pills, but it was too late. When he went in front of his black judge, he said that he had a problem and was using. They gave him six months and told him he would have to be in a rehab center. He hired a lawyer, and now he would be going straight home instead.

Six-Nine's situation was simple: he let his girl put him in prison. She lied to his PO and said he hit her. Of course, the PO believed her. Now Six-Nine was sitting in jail waiting for everything to work itself out.

"Okay! Well, hit him up when you get out and set shit up. When I come home, we will get this money. Before that, though, there are a few loose ends I need to tighten up," Lit stated, thinking about some friends that had fucked him over.

"What's that, bro?"

"Just some niggas out there running off at the mouth about shit. I can't let that slide. My BM gave me the rundown on a couple of them, so they gonna get it first. Those niggas on Turkey time right now."

"I'm here if you need me, but let's get this money, and when we see them, we'll deal with it accordingly," Hit-Man replied.

"Okay, well, I'm about to call Doja before they lock us in. She's supposed to come tomorrow. Assalamu alaikum."

"Wa alaikum salaam. I'm about to go play chess for a while," Hit-Man said, heading over to the chess table.

**

A week later, Hit-Man was sitting in the holding cell, waiting to be escorted up the hill to the bus stop. He was finally being discharged, and he couldn't wait to feel the freedom that was just a few moments away. For the past couple of days, he had been preparing himself mentally for what he was going to do.

"Grab your shit and let's go!" the CO yelled, heading for the van.

Hit-Man and eight other inmates followed the CO, trying to hurry up and get out of that place. Once they got in the van, everyone felt a sense of relief. They had seen many people get so close to leaving, but then a detainer or warrant popped up on them and kept them there. That's why no one was safe until they were outside of the wired fence.

When they reached the bus stop, they all exited the van and headed for the awaiting bus. Hit-Man was just about to get on the bus when he heard his name being called and the sound of a horn.

"Yo, Hit-Man!" the voice said.

Hit-Man stepped back to see who was calling him. When he looked at the approaching car, he smiled at the driver, then walked over to the passenger side and hopped in."What's up, cannon? What are you doing here?"

"I came to pick up Blimp, but he not getting out until tomorrow. I just got the text from his people. I was leaving when I saw you," Big Eazy stated.

"Damn, I'm glad to see you. I didn't want to be on the bus looking like this."

"What happened to your clothes?" Big Eazy said, noticing that he still had on blues.

"I don't know. They couldn't find my fucking bag, so they told me to leave this shit on. That had me hot, dawg."

"Well, here! Spark that shit up!" he said, passing him the Dutch filled with loud.

"That's what the fuck I'm talking about. I hope this is some good shit," Hit-Man said while lighting it up.

"I don't fuck with no bullshit, homie. You should know that by now. Matter of fact, you might need this," Big Eazy said, reaching inside the glove compartment and pulling out a silver .40 cal.

"What this for?" Hit-Man cocked it back, seeing if one was in the chamber.

"'Til you get back on your feet. I thought you might need it just in case niggas act stupid out here. I have to stop by my crib real quick, and then I'll take you home," Big Eazy said pulling into the apartment complex. "You can come up, bro."

Hit-Man followed Big Eazy into the building and up to the second floor. As they walked up the steps, he heard a commotion coming from what sounded like Big Eazy's apartment. As Big Eazy was about to open the door, they could hear two voices.

"Bitch! Where is the stash at, for the last time, or I'm gonna kill your friend!" the masked man said.

His partner had the girl's friend on her stomach, with a gun to her head.

She was scared to death and didn't know what to do. They had just returned from shopping, when they were ambushed and forced into the apartment. "I'm telling you the truth. I don't know where my husband keeps the stuff. I just came to pick up some money from him to go shopping later," she said hysterically.

"I'm tired of playing with these bitches!" the other dude said as he then pulled the trigger.

Boc!

The shot went straight through her back. Then he pulled out a knife and repeatedly plowed it into her. She never had a chance.

"Noooo!" the girl screamed, trying to get to her friend, but she was restrained by a swift punch to the face by the other guy. The force of the blow sent her back onto the couch.

"Silence that bitch, and let's get the fuck out of here!"

When Big Eazy and Hit-Man heard the shot, they pulled out their guns. Big Eazy didn't know if it was his wife or not, but he had to get in there. He slowly opened the door, and they could see the man with his gun aimed at the unconscious girl on the couch.

Boom! Boom! Boom! Blaca! Blaca! Blaca!

The shots found their marks, entering both intruders' bodies.

Big Eazy was the first to reach the area where the two goons had fallen. He gave both of them head shots before checking on his wife. "Soshee, are you okay, baby?" he said, holding her in his arms.

"Yo! We have to get out of here before the cops come. You know the neighbors called them," Hit-Man said, looking over at Big Eazy.

"I'll get her out of here. Can you go into the bathroom and grab the shit under the mattress?" Big Eazy asked.

Hit-Man ran into the room, and when he lifted up the mattress, he couldn't believe his eyes. There were two packages wrapped up.

Just by looking, he could tell that it was heroin. Right next to it were bundles of money. It looked like it was easily close to fifty grand. A bunch of thoughts started fluttering through his head as he grabbed the drugs and money, placing them inside of two pillowcases. As he was leaving, something caught his attention, making him think about what he was about to do.

CHAPTER 2

"Hold up! Wait a minute! Y'all thought I was finished? When I bought that Porshe, y'all thought it was rented. Flexin' on these niggas, I'm like Popeye on his spinach!" Lil' Boosie blared through the speakers as Gunz and Vick cruised down 65 South heading for Mobile.

"After we drop off this work to young bull, let's go see what's up with those niggas on that block off of Broad Street," Vick said.

"Those niggas never have any work out there. Whoever they worked for must not have a connect. We should just get a squad to run through there and take it over."

"Let's just put out some samples first to let the fiends know that we got it. Then we'll see what it do!" Vick replied.

"That's cool but fuck these niggas! They probably soft-ass young bulls."

"You need to stop thinking like that. These young bulls are the ones out here busting their guns, raising the murder rate. So, you need to watch out for them. They're trying to get their reps up. If we do that, we better be ready to lay everybody down," Vick said.

Gunz lifted up his shirt, exposing his desert eagle that was tucked into his waistband. "I'm always on go, my nigga. If they pull out, they better get the drop on me first, or they will become another casualty of the streets." He smirked.

"I feel you, cannon. I just want you to be ready for whatever. Now pass me the Amsterdam in the back seat. I'm trying to get fucked up by the time we get there. My aim is on point when I'm feeling it!"

"Say less," Gunz agreed. He took a swig of the liquor and then paused before passing it over to his homie.

By the time they made it to Mobile, they were loud and fucked up off the liquor. As soon as they turned on the block, they could see all the fiends in line waiting to cop their fix for the day. Vick pulled up in front of the door and rolled down the passenger-side window.

"Yo, homie! Come holla at me real quick," Gunz told one of the young boys.

He couldn't have been more than fifteen years old. "Give me a sec, cannon. I have to grab your bread," he replied, running up the street to the spot where they kept the cash. Their crew was told never to keep the work and money in the same spot. That way, if they were robbed or got raided, they would only lose one or the other. He came back with a black plastic bag and jumped in the back seat. "What took y'all so long to get here? You called three hours ago," Lil' Renard stated.

"Business," Vick answered. "Is it all here? The last payment was short."

"Yeah, it's all there, plus what we owe from the last one," he said confidently.

Gunz counted the money to make sure. After that, they passed him a package.

Lil' Renard smiled and tucked it under his shirt. "I'll have something for you in a couple of days," Renard told them before exiting the car.

"Yo!" Gunz said to Renard before he ran off.

Renard turned around to see what he wanted.

He passed him a smaller package. "Put that out on the streets as a tester and let us know what it does."

"What is it?" Renard asked while looking inside.

"It's some new shit that we want to see how it sells. If everything is good, we'll be switching."

"Okay, let me get back to the money," he said walking off.

"That's right! It's all about the money!" Gunz said as they pulled off.

The dope they gave Renard was all the same. The only difference was the samples were loaded with not only Quad 9 and Bonita, but also fentanyl. Vick suggested that they try something new, but never did Gunz think that he meant that way. With the chemicals that it was mixed with, the wrong dose would surely kill its user.

Their next stop was the street in the southwest area that they were talking about. The block was dead as hell, except for a couple of stragglers who were walking around. They parked in the middle of the block and just observed for a while. They wanted to see who the dealers were and what they sold. After about an hour, only a few people had come through to cop.

"I don't know about this block, bro!" Gunz said.

"It seems slow, but I really think we can move a lot of work here. All we have to do is build up the clientele, and we're set," Vick told him.

"If you say so! I'm rocking with you regardless. I was just saying that we should hold off. Let's see what the blocks around this one are doing, and then we can get an idea of what we're up against," Gunz replied.

They drove around checking out the area, and they realized that Baltimore Street all the way to Texas and Elmira was jumping. They decided the best thing to do was put a little work out and build it from the bottom up.

"Let's go check out those bitches we met the other day in West Mobile." Vick smiled. "The ones with the Truckle-gum asses?"

"Yeah. Those bitches were bad. All they want to do is smoke with us, and I know we fucking!"

"That's all it is. Then I'ma hit them up and see where they at. Hopefully they don't try to set us up. You know how those country bitches are," Vick stated as they headed over the Dolly Parton Bridge.

"This is the wrong time for niggas to try us. My trigger finger is itching," Gunz replied.

Even though he was smiling, he really was trying to catch wreck. It had been a while since they had been in a shootout. They were both born in Mobile but moved to Atlanta when they were ten years old. Their parents were trying to get them away from the violence, but that only made them hungrier for it. Vick had caught his first shooting at the age of thirteen. He was defending Gunz from a bully in school. From that day on, he would start trouble with all the thugs in his neighborhood, trying to get a rep.

Gunz only toughened up because Vick kept pushing him to fight whoever they had beef with. Now he would bust his gun in the blink of an eye. What they both didn't know was that those young bulls were on the same type of time they were. They stayed on go and didn't care who caught a slug.

They pulled up on the corner of Cottage Hill and University and waited for the chicks to come. Both of them had their guns sitting on their laps, with the safeties off. The girls came to the corner a couple miles later looking for the guys. They spotted the bombed-out boxed Chevy and walked toward it. Gunz and Vick said "Damn!" at the same time when they saw what they were wearing.

Kadeejah was wearing a pair of tights that made her ass bounce more than it should. It jiggled even more because she wasn't wearing any panties. Her T-shirt made her perky D-cup breasts sit up straight. She was short, brown skinned, and very pretty.

Her friend Jade was average in the face, tall, and had a yellow complexion. Her hair came down her back. She didn't have a fat ass like Kadeejah, but it was enough to stick out the tennis skirt she was rocking. Her double-D breasts were trying to break free from their hold in the tank top she had on.

They hopped into the backseat, and Vick turned around just in time to see in between Jade's legs. She had on a pair of pink lace panties. Her pussy lips were screaming for attention, poking out of them. That made his dick hard. "What's good with y'all?" Vick asked.

"Shit! Tryin' to get high. Y'all got some loud?" Kadeejah inquired, smacking the gum she was chewing.

"Yeah! Where we going to smoke?" Gunz asked, holding up the Ziploc bag with the loud in it.

Their eyes lit up at the sight of the trees. They looked at each other and smiled.

"My people is out until tonight. We can go to my crib and blow," Jade told them.

"That's cool, but what time they coming back, 'cause I was going to grab a bottle too so we can chill a while?"

"They won't get home from the casino until around four in the morning."

"Let's go, then. Where do you live?" Vick asked.

"I live on Cody Road. It's two blocks up and then make a right," she told him.

Vick pulled out into traffic and drove up to Jade's block. When they pulled up in front of her crib, Vick and Gunz were on alert, just in case. Seeing that the block seemed so peaceful, they relaxed.

"Come on in, y'all. Did you get any Dutches?" Kadeejah asked while getting out of her car.

"I got four games and a couple of cigarillos, so we can roll all of them up!" Gunz announced.

They walked behind the girls, thinking how they were going to fuck the shit out of them tonight. Vick pointed to the one he wanted, and Gunz laughed because he wanted the same one. When they walked into the house, the only light they saw was the flickering of the television.

"Y'all can sit at the table and roll up, and I'll be right back," Jade said as she headed upstairs.

Kadeejah turned on the kitchen light and then followed her friend up the stairs.

"I can't wait to bend that ass up!" Vick said, pulling out the bag of trees as they started breaking the Dutches open.

"I don't care who I get, as long as the pussy is good. If it's trash, I'ma let her know. You know I'm ignorant as hell!" Gunz chuckled.

"You're wild, dawg!"

Kadeejah and Jade came back downstairs, and sat up-close to the flat screen to watch Power as they chilled, geeking off of Mary J. Blige trying to act all gangsta. By the time the show was over, they were fucked up.

"Y'all want us to dance?" Kadeejah asked. She turned to one of the music channels and turned up the volume.

"Is she fucking with me, 'cause I'm fucking with you. I'm really in these streets, so what am I to do? I don't want you to leave, but if I gotta choose, I gotta keep it all the way a hundred, baby. I ain't got no time for you," PMB Rock played as the girls began dancing with one another.

Jade was so close that she could smell the Double-mint gum on Kadeejah's breath. Without saying a word, she kissed her softly on the lips. Kadeejah was hesitant at first, but she decided to play along with her friend. She had never experienced a sexual encounter with another woman before, so this was a first. She tongued Jade back passionately, and to her surprise, she felt her pussy getting wetter by the second. Her body was trembling with curiosity.

Vick and Gunz peeped what was going on and started getting ready for the show. Just as the girls started taking off their clothes, Gunz saw a shadow creeping down the stairs. He quickly reached for his gun that was tucked in the side of the couch. Vick picked up on his partner's movement and did the same.

Before the guy coming downstairs could raise his gun, Vick had the drop on him.

Boc! Boc!

Two shots hit him— one in the leg and one in his arm in which he was carrying the gun.

Kadeejah screamed at the sound of the gunfire.

"Shut the fuck up, bitch!" Gunz said, pointing the gun at them.

Kadeejah instantly quieted up. Tears were coming down her face as she stood there scared. On the other hand, Jade wasn't scared at all, which meant that she was the one who had tried to set them up.

"So, you tried to set us up, bitch!" Gunz smacked her across the head with the butt of his gun. She hit the floor face first.

Vick walked up on the nigga and hit him close range three times in the chest. "Put that scheming bitch to sleep!" Vick told Gunz.

Gunz shot Jade in the head and again in the chest. He then turned the gun on Kadeejah, who was shaking uncontrollably.

"I-I didn't know nothing about this." She sniffled.

For some reason, Vick believed her and walked over to Gunz. "Come on, man. Let the bitch be. We have to get up outta here," he whispered.

Gunz grabbed her purse and took her ID out and looked at it. "I know where you live. Keep your mouth shut, and you'll be okay."

They ran out of the house and jumped into their car, trying to get out of Dodge before the cops showed up. They got to

Government Boulevard in less than five minutes. Vick didn't take his foot off the gas until they were on 65 North.

"Yo! You were on your shit, nigga!" Vick bragged.

Gunz nodded in agreement as they headed back to the Gump. He put on his favorite song that they always played when niggas failed to get them.

"Stay schemin', niggas tryna get at me. I ride for my niggas."

Vick sparked one of the Dutches they rolled earlier and took a couple of swigs. He passed it over to Gunz, who was trying to make sure they weren't being followed. It was just something they always did. They never knew when a good Samaritan would try to take them until the cops caught up to them. He hit the Dutch and relaxed.

"Turn up that shit, homie! That's my shit!" Vick said, cruising to the music.

Gunz turned it up, and they both felt good about not getting caught slipping.

"It's funny when these stars get to acting like their broads, and every nigga's squad don't come deep with niggas like ours."

CHAPTER 3

"What looked like a robbery gone bad has left two people dead and one traumatized. We are standing outside of this South Mobile home on the fifteen hundred block of Cody Road," the reporter began, giving everyone who was watching the breaking news and all the details that had happened that night.

"Yo! Turn that up real quick. That's my block!" Slim shouted, trying to make it over to the television to catch what they were saying.

"Damn! They hit them up in the crib!" T-Baby said, holding the remote. "They left a survivor, though. They had to be some young niggas."

"I know the two people that stay at that crib. They were brother and sister, but they were some grimy muthafuckas, real talk!" Slim said as he walked away from the television.

Slim was in Atmore doing time for an armed robbery that he didn't commit. He had been walking home from Mud Bugs at the Loop, when two masked men ran past him and dropped a bag. He picked it up and found a gun along with money, and just as he tried to tuck it, two cops rode upon him. They found the evidence and locked him up.

Being from the hood, Slim knew the code of the streets, so he wouldn't say anything. They found him guilty and gave him ten to twenty years. He knew that he would beat it on appeal, so he was just waiting for his moment to get back on the streets. Someone sent him a birdie letting him know who did it. They took care of him for not saying anything, and even paid for his appeal lawyer. They also told him that they had him when he got home.

"You making the wraps tonight, or we going to eat a chee chee?" T-Baby asked.

"We can do the wraps. Just bring your stuff out, and I'll grab mine. We gotta hurry up, though, 'cause the game come on in a few."

"I know. I took Cleveland tonight. It's no way they're gonna go down three and 'o in Cleveland. Lebron is not having that!"

"You're crazy! The Splash brothers ain't even put on a show yet. What you think gonna happen once they start hitting? Cleveland might lose by forty this time!" Slim smiled.

"I got ten soups on Cleveland," T-Baby replied.

"That's a bet!" he stated.

They shook hands and went to prepare their meal before they had to lock in at nine o'clock.

* *

Lit was at Media waiting to see the judge. He was sitting in the holding cell eating the egg salad sandwich they were given when they first walked in. He and Jaleel were hopefully about to get their cases thrown out.

Jaleel was Lit's baby mom's brother. They met through her when he used to always come over. Now they were like family.

"I hope we make it back before visits start. My mom is gonna bring my son up," Jaleel said.

"Is they riding with Doja?"

"She said she was. I just want to see my lil' man. Hopefully I will be out of here today."

"Me, too. Then we won't have to get a visit. There goes your PD right there," Lit replied.

"I hope he has some good news for me. I'm not going to take anything unless it's time served."

Jaleel's PD came over to talk to him. When they were finished, the DA wanted to give him one to two years for each count running wild. That made him so mad. He told his lawyer that he would rather go to trial, and his lawyer walked away.

Lit's case was thrown out because the witnesses didn't show up again. The judge left the room for the prosecutor to recharge him once they got their shit together. They headed back to County Jail right after that.

Lit couldn't wait to get back to the streets. He had a lot of catching up to do. He hoped they released him tonight since it was still early, but it didn't matter as long as he was going home. Then he remembered that his PO still had to lift his detainer, which shouldn't be a problem being that they had dropped his case.

* *

Hit-Man was up in Norwood sitting in I-Hop eating breakfast when Trey, Corey, Derrick, and P-Funk walked in. They all sat at a table right across from him. He knew who they were but was wondering if they knew who he was. From the looks of it, they didn't or just didn't care. He got off the stool and approached them.

"You mind if I sit here?" he asked.

The three men looked up and stared at Hit-Man for a minute.

"What's up, cannon? Do we know you?" P-Funk said, sizing him up.

"It's Hit-Man, fat boy. I used to live right up the street from you."

"I don't remember you, homie. So kick rocks!" P-Funk replied in an aggressive tone.

Not wanting to start drama inside the restaurant, Hit-Man started walking away from the table.

"Bring your ass back over here, bitch boy!" Trey said with a smirk on his face.

Hit-Man turned around, and all three men were laughing at him. He smiled and sat down with them. They all gave him a fist bump and head nod.

"Where the hell have you been, nigga? You don't fuck with us bottom boys no more?" P-Funk asked.

"I've been booked, and before that, I was trying to stay out of the way."

"What brings you back around here?" Derrick inquired.

"I'm trying to get a team together 'cause I'm about to come up on a nice amount of work," he boasted.

"So, what, you trying to be a boss now?" Trey asked. He remembered Hit-Man as being the nigga always sitting on the porch drinking beer. Now he was trying to get them to work for him.

“Naw! I need you niggas to run shit for me out here while I handle shit in Biloxi and out in Mobile. We can all eat off of this. Y’all wit’ it or what?”

“So, why do you need us? What’s to stop us from just taking your shit and keeping it for ourselves?” P-Funk asked.

P-Funk never liked Hit-Man, even when he used to live around the same area. Hit-Man and him were fucking the same broad, and P-Funk got mad when she chose Hit-Man over him. The hatred had gotten to the point where P-Funk wanted to rock him, but he didn’t want to go out like that over a bitch.

“Look, man, y’all niggas been out here hustling in these streets since we were young bulls. I don’t really have experience with dope, but you do. I know you’re tired of nickels and dimes. I’m trying to put you on to some real bread. It’s every hustler’s dream to be caked up, and I’m offering you that opportunity.”

“So, where are you going to get this work from?” Derrick wondered.

“My man that I was locked up with came home and lives out in Florida with his wife. He’s gonna front me and some bull named Lit a couple of joints on consignment. All we have to do is show him that we can get this money in a reasonable amount of time. I’m just waiting for my nigga to come home now.”

“When are you getting them?” P-Funk questioned, thinking dollar signs in his head.

“It won’t be for a couple of weeks. For now, though, I have a sweet lick that we can eat off of. He holding shit. We can take some of the money from that and get some other shit until then.”

“So, who we jacking, ‘cause I need some bread right now?” Trey asked.

They stayed in the restaurant for another half hour just going over everything. He ran the whole plan over and over again so they wouldn’t forget. He knew they were hungry for a dollar, so it wouldn’t be a problem getting them to do the lick.

**

"Hurry up with my shit! You know I have to be in the crib by ten o'clock!" Blimp yelled in the kitchen to Big Eazy.

"I got you, bro. You won't be late!" he replied.

Big Eazy was watching Kayla, a Spanish woman, bag up the last bundle of dope so he could give it to his man.

Blimp had just come home three days ago and already was trying to get at some money. He had a few people left in his iPhone from before he went to prison, and he was trying to build back up.

Kayla walked into the living room to bring Blimp the bag with the bundles inside. She was only wearing a thong and a mouth protector because Big Eazy didn't trust her. Blimp took the bag from her and squeezed her ass as she walked back into the kitchen.

"You gonna take the other car, or do I have to take you home?" Big Eazy asked.

"My girl is outside waiting for me, so I'm good. I'll be over here tomorrow morning to pick up some more."

They gave each other a half hug, and Blimp left. The girl in the kitchen then walked over to Big Eazy and rubbed his crotch through his pants. His penis stood at attention, and he knew exactly what he needed. He sat down on the couch and told her to come over to him.

"Can I get a hit first? Then I will take care of you, papi," she said.

Big Eazy pulled out a needle, and Kayla licked her lips at the sight of the liquid filling inside. She took off the rubber gloves she had on, and wrapped one around her arm so that a vein would pop up. Big Eazy watched as she shot the liquid into her arm, causing her to freeze as the sensation took over her body. She was now ready for action.

She kneeled between his legs and took his dick into her mouth. The warmth of her mouth had him ready to explode. She made his dick make popping noises as she moved her head up and down while jerking on it. Big Eazy lasted as long as he could before shooting all of his load into her mouth.

"Are you satisfied, papi?" She moaned.

"I sure am! Now let's get out of here. I have to go pick up your sister from work."

She rushed and got dressed so they could leave. Big Eazy wanted to stop over at Hit-Man's crib before he picked up Soshee. That's why he needed to leave, or else he would have stayed and fucked Kayla for the great head she had just given him.

He dropped Kayla off and then stopped over at Hit-Man's place. When he pulled up, Hit-Man was sitting on the porch talking on his iPhone. Big Eazy parked and walked up onto the porch.

"What's up with you, nigga?" Hit-Man said, giving him a handshake.

"Shit! Just came to holla at you real quick. Good looking out on that shit the other day. I'm glad you were with me."

"That wasn't about shit! You're my man, dawg. I got your back."

"Let's go in the crib. I have to show you something." Big Eazy said as they both headed inside. Big Eazy pulled out a bag with around four hundred bundles and passed it to Hit-Man.

"What's this for, bro?"

"I was hoping you could handle that for me, and you can keep twenty-five percent of what you make," Big Eazy told him.

Hit-Man started adding it up in his head and realized that it wasn't a lot of money. It would only be around $7,000 while Big Eazy would pull in around $19,000. But Hit-Man decided it would do for now. "That's cool with me. I'll let you know when I have some green for you to pick up, bro," Hit-Man said.

"Alright, bet. I have to go pick up wifey. I'll get at you tomorrow, sometime."

When Big Eazy left, Hit-Man laughed at the fact that he was now being treated like the worker instead of a partner.

Not for long. Not for long at all, he thought.

CHAPTER 4

"So, you didn't tell anybody that I was home, did you?" Lit asked as they rode through Bessemer.

His PO had finally gotten him released after letting him sit an extra couple of days. The PO thought he was teaching Lit a lesson, but instead, that only made him want to get at niggas even more. His so-called friends had crossed him. Even his baby mom, who he thought loved him and worshipped the ground that he walked on, deceived him by sleeping with his man. Retribution was only a short time away.

"No! I didn't say anything to anybody, nigga! You're mine for the first forty-eight hours, and then you can go see your little friends," Doja replied.

When Doja first got Lit's call that he was getting out, she was somewhat excited and scared. She was excited that he was coming home, but she was afraid that he was coming home and that he would try to shit on her like her baby father did when he came home. Doja's problem was that she cared too much for people. She would give you her heart if you needed it. However, it seemed that the more she gave, the more people treated her poorly. She hoped that this time wasn't going to be like that. She really loved Lit and wanted a life together with him.

"You know I got you, so stop looking at me like that. Did you bring what I asked?"

She pointed under the passenger seat.

Lit reached underneath and smiled as he felt the handle to his Glock 9-millimeter. He lifted it up, cocked it to make sure one was in the chamber, and then put it back beneath the seat. "Did you do the other thing I told you to do?" he then asked, sticking his hand between her thighs, feeling her panty-less pussy.

It was shaved bald and felt smooth. She giggled and moaned at the same time as he stuck two fingers inside, making her wet. He pulled his soaked fingers out and tasted her sweet juices.

"You gonna make me crash before we get home?" she whispered, enjoying his touch.

"You need to hurry up. I got something for you!" he said, putting her hand on his dick.

She rubbed it and felt him get super hard, which only made her pussy get even wetter.

When they got to Doja's house, Lit took a shower to wash off the scent, only to add a more enticing scent—the scent of sex. They fucked for hours until he couldn't take any more. They gave each other what they both so desperately needed. Like the lyrics of Chris Brown's song says, "Lit sexed her to sleep."

Lit woke up around 11PM. He wanted to catch up to a couple of niggas before Doja woke up looking for him. He eased out of bed, grabbed her car keys, and hit the streets. Everybody that shat on him while he was down, was about to feel his pain.

He pulled up to the corner of 4th Avenue and saw a couple of familiar faces, but not the one he was looking for.

"What's good, nigga?" he said, rolling down his window.

They all stared for a minute, until one of them who recognized him spoke up. "Ain't shit! When you get out of that hell hole?"

"Earlier today. Did you see that nigga DJ today?"

"Yeah. He up the street talking to some bitch at the Chinese store. You good?" Truck stated, sensing something was up.

"Yeah. I'm straight. But if you hear something, it's only me."

Truck knew exactly what he was talking about. He gave him a head nod and finished the conversation with the young boys on the corner. Truck was one of Mobile's most ruthless killers. He already beat multiple homicides, and he wasn't afraid to bust his gun at whoever, or whenever.

Lit headed in the direction of the Chinese store. When he pulled up, DJ had his back toward him, talking to a girl he was with. Lit jumped out of the car and walked over to them. "Yo, DJ. What's good, my nigga? Let me holla at you for a sec," he said.

DJ turned around, and when he saw who it was, he got nervous. He didn't know if he should start begging for his life or run. He decided to run, but he didn't make it far. Lit pulled out his gun and shot him in the back. The girl tried screaming but caught one right between the eyes. She died before she hit the ground. Lit ran up to

DJ, who was bleeding out, and hit him again in the back of the head. Lit got in the car and peeled off to his next destination.

He pulled up past his man's crib and parked on the side street. He exited the vehicle and walked down the street, making sure no one was out before he knocked on the door. When Tru answered the door, he stared down the barrel of a gun.

"What's up, nigga? You thought I wasn't gonna find out about you fucking my BM? Back the fuck up!" Lit blurted out.

Tru held his hands up and backed up into the house. He didn't know what to do.

"Where is the work and the money?" he questioned, knowing that Tru was getting at a couple of dollars.

"It's not here, man, and I didn't know y'all were still together. I wouldn't ever disrespect you like that," Tru lied.

Tru knew they were together because he had seen her come up to visit Lit when he was on visits with his mom. When Tru got out, he saw Shaquana and told her that Lit had three other girls coming to see him every week. She got mad and tried to get back at him by sleeping with Tru. Afterward, she told Lit what she did, trying to ask for forgiveness, but he told her to fuck off.

"She told me all about the shade you threw my way. I would have never done that shit to you, dawg! Now I'm gonna ask you one more time. If you want to live, where is the shit at?"

Thinking he would be better off giving it to Lit, Tru showed him where the money and work was. He just wanted to live to see another day. He could get that little bit of shit back in no time. Lit put the stuff in a plastic shopping bag, and he then made Tru sit in a chair in his kitchen.

"Where is the rest of it, 'cause I know you had more," Lit asked.

"That's it, man! I just gave the plug his money a couple of hours ago. He was supposed to drop off something in the morning."

Lit stuck the gun under Tru's chin and threatened, "You better not be lying to me, nigga!"

Tru just wanted to get out of the situation. He was gonna kill Lit when he had the chance.

However, he wouldn't get the chance, as Lit blew his brains all over the ceiling and walls. Brain matter flew everywhere. Some blood even got on his clothes. He didn't care. Lit rushed out of the house and headed back to Doja's crib. She was still sleeping, so he eased back into bed like he had never left.

The next morning, when he woke up, he counted the money and drugs. There was only $755 and around ten ounces of loud. Lit was pissed, but he didn't care as long as that nigga was swimming with the fishes. Besides, he soon had big plans with Hit-Man. It was time to start making money.

* *

Vick and Gunz were sitting in the Kroger parking lot waiting for their connect to arrive. They had set up the meeting about a week ago, and he agreed to give them a little extra of whatever they copped.

"This nigga always late, man. We need to find a better connect," Gunz said, taking a puff off the loud he was smoking.

"I know, but right now he's all we got because of the drought. I did hear about some niggas down at the bottom, about to come up on a good plug."

"Who you hear that from, 'cause I damn sure would like to meet whoever it is."

"Some bitch said this nigga she knew told her over pillow talk that he was about to make major moves. You know niggas can't hold water when some bitch put it on them." Vick chuckled. "If you want, we can get her to set that nigga up so we can take his shit."

"I'm with it! Let me know when," Gunz agreed.

A black BMW 750 pulled up beside them and rolled down the window.

Vick had his finger on the trigger in a flash, but relaxed when he saw who it was. "What I tell you about pulling up on niggas like that? You almost got hit up again!" Vick threatened.

"You ain't hitting nothing but one of those hoochies y'all be fucking with!" Whip answered.

They all laughed and got out of their cars.

Whip gave them the bag with the one hundred bundles in it. They gave him the $5,000 and shook hands.

"I gave you the best deal I could do right now. It's fucked up out here. We need some mules that can go straight to the plug and grab the raw and uncut!" Whip said seriously.

"What about the extra you said?"

"Oh yeah, I forgot!" Whip said as he reached inside the car and gave them another twenty bundles. "That's on me, bro. I'll let y'all know if I can get my shipment here in the next couple days. If you don't hear anything from me, hit my jack."

"Cool! Be safe, you taco-eating muthafucka!" Gunz joked.

Whip gave him a crazy look before leaving. They had some more work, but they needed more. They decided to see about the nigga that the chick was talking about.

* *

Hit-Man was sitting in the car talking to Big Eazy about how the dope was selling on the block. They were so into their conversation that they didn't see the three hooded figures until it was too late.

"You niggas know what time it is? Don't fucking move, and you might just walk up outta here!" the first one said, with his gun aimed at Big Eazy's head.

"What's this all about? We don't have shit!" Big Eazy pleaded. He was pissed off because he let some niggas get the drop on him. He was usually on point.

"Shut the fuck up! Get out of the car slowly and give us the work and money, and you'll live," the second man told them.

He opened the passenger-side door and dragged out Hit-Man. The hooded man on the driver's side did the same thing to Big Eazy while the third man searched for the work. He found it in a small duffel bag. He grabbed it and nodded to his two partners. They started backing away, when Big Eazy had something to say.

"When I find out who you are, I'm gonna kill you myself and feed your bodies to my pits."

They all stopped and looked at each other. The man with the duffel bag lifted his gun and aimed at Big Eazy. Big Eazy didn't even flinch. He just grilled the guy the whole time.

Boc! Boc!

The shots hit Big Eazy in the chest, and he fell up against the car.

One of the other men pointed his gun at Hit-Man and squeezed the trigger. But the gun didn't go off. They ran away, leaving Hit-Man and his wounded friend. Hit-Man rushed over to the other side of the car to check on Big Eazy. He was just lying there, so Hit-Man thought he was dead. He hopped in the driver's seat and peeled off, leaving Big Eazy there, bleeding to death.

When they got far enough away, they removed their hoodies and gave each other a pound.

"We did that shit! I didn't think you were going to shoot the nigga, though!" Derrick said, looking into the duffel bag. "I don't know how much it is, but it looks like a lot."

"I should have hit that punk-ass nigga Hit-Man for being so disrespectful," P-Funk replied.

"You need to leave that nigga alone. He didn't do anything to your ass. As long as he doesn't open his mouth to the cops, we're cool. If he does say anything, then we'll also put his ass to sleep."

"Do you even know where you're going? You've passed the damn exit, nigga!" P-Funk said, making them all laugh.

"Fuck! We'll just get off at the next exit and cut through the park. We have to get rid of this car anyway. I'm glad we didn't take your sister's car," Trey stated as they got off at the next exit.

"She would have been pissed, especially if someone seen us leaving the scene and took down the license plate number," Derrick told them.

Once they got rid of the car, they went to P-Funk's crib. That way they could have peace and quiet as they counted the dope and money. While they were counting the money, someone knocked on the door.

"Who the fuck is that?" Derrick whispered.

P-Funk got up and peeked through the curtain to see who it was. After confirming the person's identity, P-Funk unlocked the door. He stepped to the side, allowing Hit-Man to enter.

"What the fuck did you have to shoot him for?" he asked, ice-grilling P-Funk because he knew he was the one who pulled the trigger.

"That nigga disrespected me, so he got what he deserved. Don't nobody threaten me," P-Funk replied, letting Hit-Man know not to even try it.

Derrick tried to calm the storm that was brewing. "Look! We got the money and the work, so let's get paid." He emptied the duffel bag out on the table.

Hit-Man relaxed and smiled, thinking that he had just hit a good lick. Now all he had to do was count everything and give them the work to sell. "I'll keep that little bit of cash and whatever y'all make with the dope. We'll split it four ways," Hit-Man told them, reaching for the money.

"No the fuck you won't! We split everything just like we agreed from the beginning!" Trey stated.

"It's only around nineteen-thousand there. That was some of the money he was going to give to the plug tonight. It's a lot more once we sell the dope," Hit-Man said.

"Good! We'll all split that, and then once this work is gone, we'll all be sitting a little nice. It looks like only a quarter of a brick anyway. If it's raw enough, we can cut it and almost get double its original value," Derrick told them, thinking about the numbers.

They thought it would be more work than that.

Defeated, Hit-Man took his portion of the money and left. He wasn't happy at all about the outcome, but he wasn't going to argue either. He was outnumbered and outgunned three to one. He knew their business relationship wasn't going to last too long. He just wanted to get what he could out of them first. Once they locked up most of the hood, he wouldn't need them anymore. They were just his pawns in a dangerous game of chess.

* *

"Mmmmm, oh God, no!"

Antonio heard a noise coming from his mother's room, so he and his next-door neighbor went to see if his mom was okay. As they approached the door, he could hear what sounded like his mom crying.

"Momma, are you okay?" he called to her in a mild yell.

His friend peeked through the hole on the door. He could see a man holding down Antonio's mom's hands while another man was sexually assaulting her. "We have to call the cops and get your mom some help," he said as he pulled Antonio away from the door.

Antonio yanked away from his neighbor and rushed into his sister's room. The neighbor didn't chase after him. Instead, he rushed downstairs and out the door so he could call for help.

Antonio searched in his sister's closet until he found what he was looking for. He grabbed the black box and opened it. His sister's gun was still in there. Antonio checked the clip, loaded it, and cocked one in the chamber. As he walked toward his mom's room, he heard the noise getting louder, and it sounded like one of the men was slapping her.

He pushed the door open and entered the room. The two men weren't even paying attention to him. They were caught up in their own desires. "Leave my momma alone!" Antonio yelled as tears ran down his cheeks.

One man looked up and saw the gun in his hand. He tapped his partner to get his attention. They both looked at Antonio holding the gun on them.

"Lil nigga, give me that gun before I do the same thing to you as I'm doing to your bitch-ass mom!" one of the men said, getting off the bed and heading in Antonio's direction.

Without any hesitation, Antonio squeezed the trigger of the gun. The man walking toward him caught four of the bullets. The other man tried to charge at him but was hit with two of the next barrage of bullets.

"Antonio!" his mom yelled, rushing over to him as he stared at the two bodies on the floor. When she looked into his eyes, all she saw was a blank stare. Even his tears had stopped, and no other expression was visible. She covered herself with a sheet and tried to pull her son out of the room.

Antonio was still holding the gun in his hand when the cops rushed into the house. He wasn't even scared or nervous about what he just had done. His mom was shaken up, but the two men who had raped her were dead.

"Lit!" Doja yelled, shaking him and trying to wake him up.

He jumped up in a cold sweat. He was having another nightmare. That was his third one in the last week. He didn't understand why he was having them all of a sudden.

"Are you okay?" she asked. "You're sweating all over."

"Yeah! I'm good!" he replied, getting out of bed and heading into the bathroom.

He washed his face and looked in the mirror. He was only eight years old when he first killed someone. From that day forth, he had become the menace he was today, and he didn't take shit from anyone.

He walked out of the bathroom and got back into bed with Doja.

She slid over to him and lay on his chest. She knew what was going on because he had already talked to her about it. "You know I love you, right?" she said, rubbing his arm.

"Oh, yeah? So, prove it to me then, sexy!" He smiled, pushing her head down toward his penis.

She gave him a naughty look, and then she showed him just how much. Antonio lay back and enjoyed the show.

CHAPTER 5

T-Baby and Slim were transferred to Atmore Prison because they were being classified. They were hoping they would stay in their own region so their families wouldn't have to travel too far to see them.

They were sitting in the holding cell waiting to get a pair of blues from the inmate workers, when a CO walked up to them. Everybody only had on their shoes, socks, T-shirt, and briefs.

The CO looked around at everybody and stopped when he saw an old white man with missing teeth. "What time did you wake up this morning?"

The man looked at him for a second before replying, "Three. Why?"

"Your breath smells like mints, so I was wondering," he said, sniffing the air.

"Oh, okay."

"No! No! Like you meant to brush your teeth this morning," he said, getting a laugh from everybody. The man just shook his head. Then he spotted another guy looking crazy, with his shirt tucked into his briefs. "Hold on, man. I have a serious question for you. Why do you have your T-shirt tucked into your Supermans?" he asked. "What? You trying to bring sexy back? You know what I'm doing, right? I'm just bidding off you."

He had everybody laughing at his jokes.

T-Baby and Slim just sat in the back without saying anything. They wanted to get this over with so they could get to their cell and relax. T-Baby was hoping that his appeal would hurry up and come through.

Slim already had over a year in, so he was just waiting on a green sheet from parole. "These niggas are so crazy up here. I can't wait to get out!" Slim said to T-Baby.

"Isha Allah, we both will be out of here in a couple of months. I'm trying to get back to the streets. They calling for me out there," T-Baby answered.

"I feel you, bro. Maybe we can link up and do the damn thing once we out."

"Definitely, my nigga. You already know how I get down. My brothers are out there holding shit down until I touch."

"Say no more, then!" Slim said.

Just like that, a bond was formed between the two men. Now it was just a matter of time before they would be home.

* *

"Yo! This place is jumping, bro. We might have to come through here more often," Vick said, looking at all the females sitting or dancing in their seats with hardly any clothes on.

It was hot in there, so they took off the jackets they were wearing.

"Do you see the chick yet?"

Vick looked around and scanned the area for her, but he didn't see anybody. "Naw! I think they might be running late or something."

"We should have met him down at the bottom. I don't know why he wanted to come here. Incahutes was right around the corner."

"It's cool! Let's just order some drinks and holla at some of these broads while we wait," Vick said as he ordered a drink.

Hit-Man walked into the bar with the girl a couple minutes later.

She pointed to the corner where Vick and Gunz were standing. "That's them right there. You gonna hook me up tonight, right?"

Stacy was from the south-side. She was 5'6, 140 pounds, and had a body out of this world. She was thicker until she started using dope. Everybody used to want to get at her, but she would turn them all down. Now all you had to do was hold up a couple of bags of heroin, and she'd suck the skin off your dick.

"I said I got you if these niggas give me a good offer. I didn't come here to leave empty-handed," Hit-Man replied, walking over to where the two men were standing.

Gunz and Vick watched as he and Stacy approached them. They looked at his appearance and thought it was a joke. Hit-Man had on a pair of Guess jeans and a Polo T-shirt.

"That nigga don't look like he's getting money with that old-ass shit on." Vick smirked.

"Chill out, my nigga. Let's hear what he has to say first before we start judging."

"Okay. But if it's some bullshit, I'ma smoke his ass soon as he leaves this joint."

"What's up, fellas? Stacy tells me that you're trying to find a good connect. How much are you trying to grab?" Hit-Man asked.

"I'm not trying to discuss business here. You never know who's listening," Gunz stated as he looked around.

"That's the reason I chose this place. The music is loud enough where we can talk regular, and no one can hear us unless they're right here."

Vick agreed after taking everything into consideration. He knew that Hit-Man was right, so he asked him a question. "How much work can you get at one time, and is it any good?"

"I can assure you that the quality is very good. I can let Stacy here prove it to you if you like," he said, holding up a bag so she could see it. "And I can get you whatever amount you need."

"Cool! Let her try it out then," Gunz replied.

Stacy's mouth was watering at the thought of getting the high she'd been craving all night. Hit-Man passed it to her, and she scurried off toward the ladies' room. She already knew that it was some good dope, but Hit-Man had told her he would give her something, so he kept his word.

She returned from the bathroom ten minutes later. Her eyes were half closed, and her speech was slurred as she told them how it was. "That is some good dope!" She sat down in one of the chairs and was nodding in and out.

Vick and Gunz smiled at each other thinking how they would come up off of this. They were even still going to mix it with the fentanyl for the extra boost. Hit-Man was also smiling, but not for the same reason. He was going to cut the dope he had, to be able to give them what they needed. Even though it was cut twice, he also knew that it would still have a lot of kick with the fentanyl.

"We want to start off with four hundred bundles, if that's not too much for you." Gunz smirked. He thought Hit-Man wouldn't be able to get that amount of dope, which was actually a lot more than what they were able to get right now. They only had about 30 bundles left from the 120 they got from Whip. They tried to get more, but he wasn't able to right now.

"That's not a problem! Just have that money for me in a couple of days. I'll at least need until tomorrow, and I'll call you with the meeting spot. Is that cool with you guys?"

Gunz and Vick had no choice but to agree. They needed work now because the new street was really starting to pick up now.

"Here's the number you can reach me at. Just call when you're ready to do business. I hope it's not much longer because we have plenty of buyers waiting," Vick said, passing him a piece of paper with his cell phone number on it.

Hit-Man took the paper, and they shook hands. Just like that, a deal had been made, and now it was up to Hit-Man to make sure he delivered.

He waited for another ten minutes after they had left before he left. He had to get back down to the bottom and try to get whatever they were holding, because he needed that to go with what he had. He couldn't wait for his Florida plug to come through so he would be ready when Lit got home. He knew that once Lit was out, they would be unstoppable in the drug game.

He still was going to hit every lick that came his way, with the help of his little crew he had formed. What he didn't know was that Lit was already home. He was just lying low and making sure no one would be on his ass before he got up with Hit-Man.

* *

Lit was sitting in the crib watching ESPN, when he received a phone call. He picked up his iPhone from the nightstand and looked at the screen. "Yo, Truck! What's good, my nigga?" he said, answering it.

"Ain't shit. Can you talk right now?"

"Yeah. I was just watching this shit about Durant. That nigga really just left OKC to go to Golden State."

"Wouldn't you do that shit just to play with the Splash brothers?" Truck stated. "Anyway, shit has been hot around here ever since you handled your business with ol' boy. I think somebody is talking, but they not saying you. They blaming it on some niggas from the Gardens, so, my nigga, you in the clear!"

"That's good to know. Now I can hit up my homie and get to the money. I was tired of sitting around the crib all day."

"Well, just look out when you get some work. Shit has really been dry around here," Truck stated.

"I have a little something for you right now if you want it. Come to my girl's spot in like twenty minutes."

"What is it?" Truck questioned.

"Loud," Lit answered, thinking about the work he took from Tru.

"Okay, cool! But I'm talking real work. I'll see you in a few, 'cause I don't like speaking about shit on the jack."

"I feel you, and I'll get at you when you get here."

Lit ended the call just in time to catch the end of ESPN. They were talking about how Lebron and Cleveland should try to sign D. Wade to help match up against the Warriors. They even mentioned Gasol's name, too.

He laughed as he sipped on some Hennessy. He jumped when he heard the front door slam.

A couple of seconds later, Doja walked in, staring at Lit like she was ready to kill him. "I thought you didn't fuck with your baby mom anymore?" she asked, throwing her keys at him, just missing his head.

"What are you talking about?"

"Don't fucking play dumb with me, Antonio. I've stuck by you the whole time you were locked up, and this is how you repay me!" she said, pulling up something on her phone and showing it to him.

Lit read the message that Shaquana had posted on Facebook, and then Doja showed him the video of them on Snapchat.

She was so upset, tears started falling from her eyes. Lit knew he had fucked up by taking pictures of him and his family. He didn't want to hurt Doja because she had done so much for him.

"Come here, baby. I'm sorry about that. I didn't know she was going to post that. All I did was go see my kids. You can understand that, can't you?" he asked, trying to calm down the situation.

"If you wanted to still be with her, why didn't you say so? I would have fell the fuck back. I feel like you were just using me for money." Doja was a good, ambitious twenty-five-year-old, but at that minute she felt like committing murder. People always took her kindness for weakness. Lit tried to put his arms around her, but she pushed him away. "Why would you do this to me?" she yelled.

"I told you, nothing's going on between us. If you don't believe me, then fuck it. I'm out of here!" He started getting dressed and then headed for the door.

Doja ran in front of him and blocked the entrance. She would not move out of his way. "You're not going anywhere. You're gonna stay here and tell me what I want to know."

"Get out my way. I need some air!" he stated, pushing her to the side. He walked out the door and headed up the street. He didn't have a car yet, so he just walked around for a while.

Truck pulled up alongside him and rolled down the window. "What's up, nigga? Where the hell you going?"

Lit walked over to the car and hopped inside. He leaned the seat back a little, pulled out the bag of loud, and passed it over to Truck. "I had to get out of the crib for a few. Doja's tripping about me going to the playground with my kids and their mother."

"Why she tripping about that? You gotta see your kids."

"Man, Shaquana posted that shit on the 'Book and Snapchat. Now Doja thinks I'm still fucking her," Lit replied.

"Damn, nigga! I know you're bloody about that. Well, I'm going to the crib. Do you want to come chill and blow?"

"Naw! I'm about to go back home and get shit straight with her. Can you take me out to Mobile tomorrow? I have to get up with the bull Hit-Man, so we can get shit poppin' out here. It's money to be made!" Lit said.

"I got you. Just hit my jack when you're ready, and I'll swing through."

"Cool! I'll get at you then," he said, opening the door to get out.

"How much is this, and what you want back?" Truck asked, holding up the package.

"It's ten ounces, and just give me fifteen hundred back, and you keep the rest. I have some bigger shit going on if you trying to really get at some money. I'll be linking up with a real plug in a day or two."

"Well, like I said, I need some work, so let me know what's up. I'm with you," Truck said as he started to get excited.

"I'll hit you up in the AM, then," Lit said as he walked away toward his house.

It was time to get the money, and nothing was going to stop him.

* *

When Lit got back home, it was too quiet. He walked into the bedroom, and it looked like a tornado had hit. Clothes were thrown all over the place, and Doja lay in the bed sniffling from crying. Lit walked over to where she was and pulled her to the edge of the bed. He opened her legs, pulling her panties to the side, and began to finger her pussy.

She wanted to object, but it felt too good. Her pussy was getting wetter and wetter by the second. "Stop! I'm mad at you, nigga!" She moaned, spreading her legs wider for him.

He knew she didn't want him to stop, so he stuck another finger inside and then another, until he was fucking her with three fingers. He even stuck his thumb inside her ass, which caused her to cum instantly. That was only the beginning, as he started sucking on her clit.

By this time, Doja wasn't even thinking about the argument they had earlier. She needed to feel him inside her. "Oh, baby. I need some dick right now, please!" she begged, holding his head between her legs.

Lit stood up, knowing that he had her where he wanted her. He took off his clothes and gave her what she needed for the next two hours. By the time he was done with her, she had fallen right to sleep, forgetting about everything that had happened.

CHAPTER 6

Beep! Beep! Beep! Beep!

The respirator machine that Big Eazy was hooked up to made a continuous sound.

He was in critical but stable condition after taking two bullets to the chest. The men who shot him thought he was dead because he lay still on the ground until they left. He thought at least his friend Hit-Man would help him, but he took off too. That left a sour taste in his mouth. However, he told himself that if the roles were reversed, he probably would have done the same thing.

Soshee stayed in the room with her man, not leaving his side except to use the bathroom or get something to eat. She wanted to go home and take a quick shower, but she didn't want to miss anything going on with his condition. They talked briefly the previous night, before the medicine knocked him right back out. She leaned her head back on the chair, trying to catch a quick nap, but was interrupted by the sound of the door opening.

The doctor walked in with a clipboard in her hand. "Hello! Are you awake?"

"Yes!" Soshee replied, standing up and stretching. "When will he be able to go home?"

"Well, that's the good news I came to give you. Everything looks normal," the doctor told her, looking at Big Eazy's chart. "His wounds are healing nicely, and there's no sign of infection. You can take him home today if you want."

Excitedly, Soshee nodded. Her man had been cooped up in that hospital too long. She needed to get him home where he could relax in the comfort of his own bed.

"Come with me so you can sign his release papers, and once he wakes up, you can take him home."

Soshee gave Big Eazy a kiss on the cheek before following the doctor to sign the discharge papers. She hoped he would be awake by the time she returned, or she was going to wake his ass up herself. She wanted to get out of there ASAP.

As if on cue, when Soshee returned, Big Eazy woke up with a groggy look on his face. He looked around the room like he was looking for something.

"Hey, baby, what's wrong?" she asked.

"Where are my clothes? I'm getting out of here before they try to keep me any longer."

"I just signed the papers, so you can come home now anyway, daddy. I got your clothes right here," she said, lifting up the shopping bag.

Thirty minutes later, they were in Soshee's car heading home. She made a few stops on the way, at Walmart and Sneaky Pete's. She had to get his prescription filled and buy some bandages. They also got a couple of sandwiches because she didn't want to cook.

When they got in the house, Big Eazy sat down on the couch. "Did you hear anything from Hit-Man and Blimp?" he asked, scrolling through his phone.

"Blimp called several times checking up on you, but I only heard from Hit-Man the one time I told you about. When I tried to call him back to let him know that you were okay, he never answered the phone. I would have left a message or texted him, but my only concern at the time was you."

"That's okay, momma. I'll hit him up in a few. Right now I need to talk to Blimp," he said, pressing send on his iPhone. He wanted to find out if niggas were talking about coming up on some work. His work! Whoever was behind his attempted murder and robbery was going to pay.

Blimp didn't answer, so he left a voice message. Big Eazy knew that once he saw the number, Blimp would surely hit him right back. His next call was to Hit-Man.

After a couple of rings, Hit-Man picked up. "Yo, who this?"

"This Big Eazy, my nigga! What's good?" he asked.

"Stop playing with me. My nigga Big Eazy got slumped by some bitch-ass nigga. So, if you got his cell phone, when I find you, you're dead!" he said, making it seem like he was serious and unaware it was his friend.

Hit-Man knew it was Big Eazy. He had heard from one of his friends that he had survived the shooting. However, he didn't want to go visit him because he didn't know what to say. Eventually, he knew this call would be coming, so he wanted to see where Big Eazy's head was.

"This Big Eazy, man, I'm still breathing. They need to hit me more than twice for me to check. Why did you leave me like that for dead, bro? I wouldn't have left you."

"Man! Shit was crazy that day. I thought they were going to kill me, too, but the gun jammed. If I would have known that you were still breathing, I would have helped you out. I heard the cop sirens and got out of there. I even looked for your gun since you're always strapped," he lied.

Big Eazy believed him, but there was just something about the way he said it that caused a little bit of doubt. "So, where you at now?"

"Down at the bottom trying to get this money so I can get some work. Shit has been dry lately, man. Do you know where I can get something from?" Hit-Man asked. Hit-Man had work already, but he didn't want Big Eazy to know that it was his work that was going around.

"I don't know yet. I have to see what's up with my cousin. He knows what happened to me, and I know he's still gonna want his money. Let me get back to you on that. Be safe out there, nigga. I'm about to eat with my girl."

"Okay, you too, bro! Just hit me up when you want me to swing past there."

"Cool! Did Lit touch yet?"

"I don't know. I'll call his people and see what's good."

"Alright, cannon. See you later!" Big Eazy said, ending the call.

After calling his cousin and letting him know that he was out of the hospital, he and Soshee ate their food while watching a movie. Soshee wanted some dick, but she didn't want to hurt Big Eazy, so she just gave him some head, and he played with her pussy until they both exploded. He promised that he would blow out her back in a couple of days when he was fully recovered. She couldn't wait either.

CHAPTER 7

Lit and Truck made it to Mobile just as rush hour was starting. Lit only had one thing on his mind, and that was getting money. He wasn't broke, but he definitely wasn't comfortable either. He didn't even have his own car yet, so he depended on his girl or his niggas to take him everywhere. The bus was not an option because he was always strapped. Being without his gun was like being without his dick. People would think he was a pussy and try to stick him.

They pulled up on the avenue looking for Hit-Man. As they slowly drove down the block, niggas out hustling or playing craps looked up. They didn't recognize Truck's car, so an alert went up. Were they cops or niggas trying to stick them? Lit noticed the tension and placed his gun under his leg, just in chase shit got ugly. Truck already had his .40 caliber out and had taken the safety off. He rolled down the window and showed that he came in peace.

"Yo, cannon! I'm just looking for my man Hit-Man. We was locked up together in Atmore," Lit said.

"Hit-Man ain't around here. That bitch-ass nigga up the street somewhere. Take y'all nut asses out of here before shit get crazy!" one of the young bulls said, lifting up his shirt and exposing his 9-millimeter.

Two of his goons did the same thing, trying to impress a couple of chicks standing beside them.

"No doubt, bro!" Lit said, signaling for Truck to pull off.

"Yeah, roll the fuck up outta here, and don't come back," another one yelled. He threw a bottle, hitting Truck's back window.

Truck stopped abruptly and backed up his car. All the young boys standing out there suddenly stood up. If they only knew who they were fucking with, they would have scattered immediately. Truck jumped out with an AR-15, and Lit had a shottie, which he'd had in the backseat.

"Move, and I'ma light this fucking block up like the Fourth of July!" Truck yelled. "Which one of you bitch-ass niggas threw a bottle at my shit?"

None of them responded, so Lit smacked the closest one to him in the face with the back of the gun, causing him to fall to the ground. Four of his teeth fell out along with some blood. One of the other lil niggas tried to pull out on them, but Truck was on him.

Blaca! Blaca! Blaca!

He hit him with the assault rifle, instantly killing him. Nobody else dared to move. They put their hands in the air. One of them even pissed himself because he was so frightened.

"I'm only going to ask one more time, and then all of you are gonna lay the fuck down!" Truck said, with murder in his eyes.

Hit-Man was turning the corner when he saw one of the young bulls drop dead from the shots. He was about to run the other way until he recognized one of the dudes. "Yo peeps, what's going on?" he asked as he was walking toward the group.

Lit spun around, ready to let go with the pump, until he saw who it was.

"These niggas are disrespectful and need to be taught a lesson," Truck suggested.

"The police station is right up the street. Let's get out of here," Hit-Man said, hopping in the backseat of the car. "Come on, man! The cops are probably on their way."

Truck and Lit jumped into the car and peeled off as Hit-Man directed them to his crib on Tanglewood Drive.

Not trying to get caught, the young boys scattered down the street. They were happy that their lives had been spared for the moment.

"Nigga, when did you get home?" Hit-Man asked Lit while giving him a pound.

"I've been out for a few. What's good though with the bull? Did you talk to him yet?" Lit asked.

"I hit him a couple days ago, and he said everything was in place. He was just waiting for you."

Lit figured he didn't want to deal with Hit-Man, which is why he told him that. He decided he would hit him up ASAP so he could make some money. "How many blocks do you have out here so far? I'm trying to flood all of them with some work."

"We got Cameron Circle, but that block will be hot for a while now because of the body. I also have a couple of blocks in the southwest that we can use. These two young bulls from Chicago be DJing out there. I just had a meeting with them about copping from me. They can just DJ for us," Hit-Man told them.

"Okay! Well, I'm going to chill out this way for tonight. I have to go see this chick that keeps hitting my phone. She's about getting paper, so I'm gonna put her on the team. I'm trying to hit up the Palladium afterward so I can see what all this talk is about. You rolling?" he asked Hit-Man.

"Hell yeah! Just hit my jack when you ready. I also might have a couple more blocks. I'll let you know about that tomorrow," Hit-Man stated, thinking about Ensley.

"Those niggas still got my blood, dawg. I need to relieve some tension, so I'll stay out here with you," Truck said.

"Well, we'll get at you when we're ready to roll out," Lit said to Hit-Man as he and Truck headed out the door.

They shouldn't have stayed around there anyway since they had just murked a nigga. They looked around cautiously before jumping in the car and peeling off.

"I'm not going to show my face around there for a while. Somebody might have said something," Truck said as he headed out of Fairfield.

CHAPTER 8

Chloe was sitting on the steps getting her hair braided from some shortie she met out in the Southwest. She needed her shit tight for when she and her crew hit the club later.

"So, are you still gonna kick it with me tonight when you get back?" Peaches asked.

"Definitely! If your sexy ass is still up when I get out of there," Chloe replied, sticking her hand between Peaches's legs and playing with her pussy.

Peaches had to stop doing her hair for a minute because Chloe had her pussy soaked, and she could feel her juices seeping through her panties. "You have to stop that if you want me to finish your hair." Peaches moaned, with her eyes closed.

Chloe grew up in Pelham on Clay Street. She had been living out there most of her life. Growing up around five brothers made her tough as nails. She could hang with the toughest nigga around, blow for blow, and wouldn't back down. With all the toughness that she demonstrated, no one got to see the feminine side of her. Without a doubt, she was a dime piece.

She stood 5'7" and weighed 130 pounds. She had a caramel complexion, a small waist with a fat ass, and D-cup breasts that she kept stuffed under her sports bra. When she wore some sexy clothes, no chick in Birmingham was fucking with her. She preferred to dress like a tomboy, though, and that still didn't hide the fact that she was bad. She was bisexual, though, so both men and women had their chance with her.

"Okay! I'ma chill out so you can finish. I'm tearing that ass up later, though."

Peaches just smiled and finished doing her braids.

When she got close to being done, Chloe stood up to stretch. She turned to say something to Peaches, when she felt cold steel against the back of her head.

"You know what it is. Give that shit up or lay down!" the voice said.

Chloe didn't even flinch, but Peaches was scared as hell. Chloe just shook her head. "I'm not giving up shit, so do what you gotta do!" Chloe replied.

Lit laughed as he took the gun from her head and tucked it under his shirt. "I caught your ass slipping, didn't I?"

"Not really, cannon," she said, looking down toward his dick. "I'm always on point."

Lit looked down and noticed the .25 aimed at his shit. He shook his head in disbelief at how on point she was. They gave each other a hug as Truck stepped out of the car. Lit then introduced them to each other, and they gave a head nod to one another.

"I told you niggas ain't fucking with her," Lit bragged to Truck.

"She's the real deal!" He smiled.

"But anyway, Chloe, I need to holla at you on some real shit," Lit said, with a more serious look on his face.

"What's up?"

"I want you to get down with us on some get messy shit. I know you do your boosting thing, but I need someone like you to run Cahaba Heights for me. All you have to do is collect the money and make sure nothing comes back short. If you need a gun or manpower, just give me a call."

Chloe stood there for a minute to take it all in. She had never sold drugs before, and as tempting as his offer was now, she needed more time to think about it before making her decision.

"Let me give it some thought for a day or two, Lit. You know I'm more into other shit than that, but I will give you an answer. Right now, though, I'm trying to get ready for the club," she stated, rubbing her hands together. "What you niggas getting into tonight?"

"We going to the Palladium. Which one are you going to?"

"The same place. Y'all trying to roll deep with me and my girls, or what? We won't cock block you," she told him, giving him a nudge with her elbow.

"We can do that, baby girl. Just make sure you dress to impress. Of course, we are," Lit replied, heading for the car.

"Don't worry. We will be."

When they got back on the road, Lit decided it was time to give bull a call and set things in motion. By this time next week, he was hoping to have more dope than anybody else around.

* * *

The Paladium was packed by the time Lit, Truck, Chloe, and the rest of her lil crew arrived. Lit and Truck pulled up in a rented 2022 Audi 8, and Chloe and three other girls were in a 2022 Acura RL. The car belonged to one of the girl's brothers, who was getting at a couple of dollars. He purchased it from a chop shop out in the Northeast.

Lit had on a fresh pair of Butters, True Religion jeans, and a fitted T-shirt that made him look cut up. Truck had on similar attire; the only difference was that he rocked all-black everything. He stayed on his grimy shit just in case muthafuckas got out of pocket.

Chloe stepped out of the car in a Chanel dress that came just above the knee, and a pair of five-inch stilettos that wrapped around her leg up to her thighs. Her individual braids flowed down her back. She had on costume jewelry that looked so real that it sparkled from the light.

Her friend Latisha wore a strapless Christian Dior pencil dress and four-inch stilettos. She had long, straight hair that came almost to her ass, because of her heritage. She was Black and Puerto Rican and had emerald eyes. She stood 5'7 and weighed 120 pounds. She had perky C-cup breasts and a nicely proportioned ass that made her figure perfect.

Lena had a caramel complexion and juicy lips. She had on a low-cut black dress with the back out. It was so short that if she moved the wrong way, her whole ass would be exposed. She had on three-inch red pumps, with a matching purse. She was biracial as well, a mixture of Black and Jamaican.

Last but not least was Melody, who was the thickest of the crew. She stood 5'4 and weighed 142 pounds. She had DD breasts and short hair. Melody had on a pair of Apple Bottoms jeans with a tight fitted shirt, letting everyone know she had big perky titties underneath. She never sported a bra, and they still sat straight up. She wore thigh-high boots, with the jeans tucked inside of them.

All the women were indeed dressed to impress. They had niggas gawking as they all headed to the VIP section. The server brought over two complimentary bottles to the group.

"The owner says these are on the house," she told them, setting the bottles on the table. She looked at the group of women and gave them a seductive smile before glancing at Lit. "He would like to talk to you in his office for a minute."

Lit didn't even know the owner, so he wondered what this was about. Curiously, he got up and followed her upstairs, through a couple of doors, and into the office, where two men were talking while looking out at the crowd. Once the server stepped out and closed the door behind her, they introduced themselves.

"Hello, Antonio!" one man said, calling him by his real name. "My name is Miguel, and this is Quincy."

They both shook Lit's hand before inviting him to sit down. Wanting to get down to business so he could get back to the fun downstairs with his friends, Lit said, "So, what did you need to see me for, and thanks for the bottles."

"You're welcome, chico. And it seems that we have a mutual friend," Miguel began. "You talked to my father's partner earlier about getting some work on consignment."

Lit only talked to one person earlier, and it was only briefly because they didn't want to discuss anything over the phone. He wondered how the hell they knew that.

Miguel saw the look of confusion on Lit's face and decided to calm his suspicions.

"No, we are not cops, feds, or any other law enforcement agency. My dad's name is Felipe, and his partner is C.J. He called me earlier today and told me you would be coming here tonight. That's why you and your friends are getting the red-carpet treatment."

"Wait! So C.J. told you to hook us up?" Lit asked, not really believing him.

"Yes, he and my father are in Vegas. I control everything on this side for them. If you don't believe me, I can put you on speaker phone right now," Miguel stated, holding the phone handset up for Lit.

At that moment, Lit realized just how big C.J. really was. He had ties to the Mexican cartel. Lit felt like he had just cashed in on something big.

"That won't be necessary," Lit replied, with a slight grin on his face, thinking about dollar signs.

"Okay, well I know you want to finish enjoying yourself, so this is for you," Quincy spoke up and said, passing him a cell phone. "Something will be arriving at your girlfriend Doja's house in the morning, or would you like it to go to your baby mom Shaquana's house?"

Lit looked up in surprise when Quincy said Doja's and Shaquana's names. They knew more about him than he did about them. He just shook his head.

"Doja's house is cool. I'll be there waiting when it arrives. But what time will it be there?" He questioned.

"Around noon. Is that okay?" Quincy asked.

"Yeah, that is cool."

"Okay. Well, it will be two keys of pure heroin. The going price for it is $75,000 a key. Since we are giving it to you on consignment, that price stands. How fast will you be able to move that kind of work?" Miguel asked.

"I, or should I say we, can start as soon as we get it. I don't see it being a problem. I have a good team that I just put together. Me and my partner, Hit-Man, will have Mobile and Birmingham popping in no time."

"Okay, great. We will only deal with you, though, not your friend. You should be careful around him too," Quincy warned.

Lit brushed it off, not even thinking about what they just said about Hit-Man. He was just glad to finally have a connect. The men talked for about ten more minutes before Lit went back down to the VIP section with his friends. Tomorrow would be the start of business, but tonight was his time to have fun.

* * *

Hit-Man arrived at the club an hour late. He told Lit to meet him there because he had something to do.

He and Derrick were staking out a spot owned by a couple of bikers. Someone told him they were sitting on major paper and drugs. Hit-Man wanted it all, so they had been watching them for a week. They wanted to wait for about a month before going in. That way they would have their whole routine down pat.

After getting frisked by the bouncers, Hit-Man and Derrick made their way over to the VIP section where Lit, Truck, and the girls were drinking and enjoying the strippers.

"What's up, nigga?" Hit-Man said, greeting Lit with a half hug.

After everyone was introduced, Hit-Man poured himself a drink.

"Yo. Everything is a go on that situation," Lit whispered to Hit-Man as a thick white girl gave him a lap dance.

"That's what's up, so when will we be set?"

"Tomorrow."

"Okay. What's up with these shorties you with?" He asked, staring at Chloe and her crew.

"They're off limits, bro. They are a part of the team," Lit told him.

Hit-Man just nodded but kept staring at one girl in particular. Lena's ass was bouncing as she danced to the music. His dick got hard just from staring at the thong that was swallowed up by her cheeks. The strippers were there for the night, courtesy of Quincy and Miguel, but all he wanted was her.

"We'll be back. We're going over to the stage to make it rain on these bitches," Chloe said to Lit, leading her friends out of the VIP area.

"So, what's really the deal with you and Chloe?" Truck said, trying to get the scoop.

"Nothing. I helped her out of a jam a while ago. She almost got pickled trying to steal at Victoria Secrets at the Galleria Mall, and I got her up out of there."

"Damn. You saved her ass. So now she's been loyal to you. So, what will they be doing?" Truck asked.

"Working," Lit said, giving Truck a crazy look. "This ain't no free ride for anybody. We all got to do our parts."

"Well, if you need me, bro, you know where—" Truck couldn't finish his sentence because he noticed some shit about to pop off by the stage. "Why that nigga keeps trying to grab homegirl?"

Lit looked over toward the stage to see some dude smack the shit out of Lena. Before he could stand all the way up, Chloe dropped the nigga with a bottle to the back of his head. She and the other girls started stomping him on the ground. A few of his boys started rushing over toward them.

"Let's go!" Lit said, rushing through the crowd, with Truck and Hit-Man on his heels.

One dude tried to swing but was quickly put on his ass with a haymaker from Truck. Lit gripped one of the other niggas by the collar, pulling down his face and kneeing him in the mouth. Blood flowed everywhere. People in the crowd watched the fight in awe, until about fifteen bouncers rushed in, grabbing the niggas and tossing them out. Lit and Chloe helped Lena to the ladies' room to fix herself up. Lit stayed by the door until they came out. Even though they didn't have to leave, they wanted to get the fuck up outta there.

"We're going to head home so I can make sure that she gets in the house safe. Are you staying out this way tonight or going back out to Mobile?" Chloe asked Lit.

"I have some shit to take care of, so I'm going home. Are you good?"

"Yeah, I'm good," she replied, lifting up her dress a little to show him her gun that was strapped to her leg.

"I don't even know why I asked," Lit said, shutting the door after she got in. "Y'all ladies take care, and I'll hit your jack tomorrow."

"Okay. And I'm with you on that thing we talked about too. Me and my girls can handle shit out there."

"Say no more," he said, watching as the ladies pulled off.

He rushed over to the car so he could get home as quickly as possible. He knew that Doja was going to flip out. She didn't even call to see where he was at. That right there told him that he was in trouble.

CHAPTER 9

The four hundred bundles that Vick and Gunz had copped from Hit-Man went in no time. They needed more because the fiends loved that shit. It was around ten o'clock in the morning when they met up with Hit-Man at the BP on Dixon. Hit-Man and Derrick pulled into the station a couple minutes later and parked on the side right next to them. Hit-Man got out and jumped into the backseat of their car.

"What's good with you, nigga?" Gunz said, giving him a nod.

"Shit, you know me, just trying to get this money. My man is meeting up with our plug right now, so I will have something ready for y'all by tonight."

"I thought you had something for us now. We could have waited 'til later," Vick replied, with frustration.

"Yeah, Hit-Man, we told muthafuckas we would be back up within an hour. Now they might try to cop from someone else," Gunz added.

"I have something to hold you off for now if you want it?" He replied. "Or you can get in on this lick that me and my man's about to handle today."

"What you talking about?" Vick asked, interested.

"We've been watching this spot for a while now, and these niggas is getting money. I'm trying to hit them today while they still have everything there. It's only a couple of them there in the morning, so we can be in and out."

"Why you want to hit these niggas in broad daylight? That shit is too risky. What if people see us and call the cops?" Gunz asked.

"Trust me. Ain't nobody gonna be around this place, and they sure as hell not calling no pigs. Two of my homies are out there now waiting for us. So are y'all in or out?"

Both Vick and Gunz looked at each other momentarily, thinking about the situation. The look in their eyes said it all without even speaking. If this nigga tried some funny shit, they were going to lay his ass down, and whoever was with him. They wanted that bread, so they agreed to go with them.

"Follow us to the spot so we can go over the plan and load up. We have heat, so y'all don't have to use your own shit," Hit-Man said, stepping out of the car.

"We good on that part. I only use my shit. That way there are no problems," Vick told him.

"Suit yourself. Let's get this money."

Hit-Man walked back over to the car and hopped in with Derrick. He gave him a head nod, which indicated that the two men were in. Derrick smiled and pulled off, with Vick and Gunz following.

* * *

When Lit had returned home last night, Doja wasn't even there. He walked into the bedroom and noticed that most of her stuff was gone. He figured she was tired of his shit and left him. He didn't care, because all that was on his mind was getting back up. As he sat on the edge of his bed in a wifebeater and boxers, he thought about what kind of money they would be bringing in off of the work, and a smile crept across his face. His thoughts were interrupted by a knock on the door.

Lit quickly threw on a pair of shorts and headed downstairs. When he looked through the peephole, a guy was standing there in a FedEx uniform. Thinking that it was a package for Doja, Lit opened the door.

"What's up, man?"

"Good morning, sir. I just need you to sign right here, please," the delivery man said, passing him the tablet.

Lit quickly signed and took the package from him. When he looked down at the name on the address, he looked back up at the man.

"I didn't order shit."

"Mr. Miguel said that he will contact you later and that you will be pleased with the contents," the man said before walking away, getting inside the van, and pulling away.

Lit already knew what it was, and a smile grew on his face. It was time to get paid. He opened the box, and the first thing he saw was a cell phone. He removed it, along with the plastic that was concealing something at the bottom. He pulled out three packages and sat them on the table. He was only expecting two, so when he saw the third one, he realized what the delivery man meant.

He called Truck to come pick him up so they could get to Mobile to start bagging up. That's why he needed Chloe's friends. She would be in charge of that part. After he hung up with Truck, he called Chloe to inform her that he would be there in an hour and a half. He got dressed and ate a bowl of cereal before Truck arrived.

* * *

Two hours later, they were sitting in Chloe's kitchen. Lit removed one of the packages from the book bag he was carrying and sat it on the table. Truck and Chloe pulled up two chairs and sat next to him, to get a better look at the work. Lit pulled out his pocketknife and dug into a corner of the brick to open it up. The three of them looked at the brown block and frowned up their faces in a puzzled look. They had no idea that heroin was brown like that. It was so brown that it almost looked like chocolate.

But Lit remembered Miguel and Quincy saying that he would be getting raw dope, but that was an understatement. That shit was almost pure. Lit knew he could probably cut it seven times, but he was only going to do it five times. That way they would more than triple their money and wouldn't kill friends in the process. People would surely leave the other dealers alone and only fuck with them once they tasted it.

"This shit is crazy," Chloe said, looking at the brick. "What do you need me to do?"

"Have your girls come over and help cut, bag, and stamp everything up. That's what you're in charge of. You can also drop off when the corners get low or have one of them do it. Is that cool with you?" Lit asked.

"Hell yeah. They are upstairs chilling right now. I'm gonna call them so we can get started," Chloe replied, heading for the stairs.

"Chloe!" Lit yelled, stopping her before she reached the top of the steps. "They have to wear masks and gloves. And the only clothes they can have on is their panties. I don't want no one trying to take my shit. Is that cool?"

"For that money, these bitches will walk around this muthafucka butt naked and twerking their asses in the process," she replied, smiling at Lit.

"Well, go get them so I can show them how I want it done. Then, we're gonna set up shop and get paid."

"This shit is going to have niggas on their backs," Truck stated, looking at the brown brick.

"That's the idea, bro. So, start opening that up while I get the bags and shit ready and call Hit-Man."

Lit wanted to move the work a little differently. They would sell it by the gram or the bundle. The grams would go for $60, as would the bundles. A smart person would buy the gram, and they could get almost two-and-a-half bundles, but that would be unlikely. People were so anxious and in a rush to get high, and blinded by reality, that they were only getting fourteen bags in a bundle for sixty dollars and didn't even see the benefit in buying a gram. It didn't really matter to Lit how they got it, though, as long as the money was coming in.

He spent the next two hours showing the girls how to bag and stamp the heroin. He even showed them just how much cut to put on it, using the fentanyl so they didn't fuck the money up. After the first hour, you would have thought they had been doing it all their lives. They had it down to a science and Lit enjoyed the fact that he could go handle other things while they were doing that.

"Chloe, me and Truck got some shit to take care of. If you need me, just hit my jack."

"Cool. You gonna drop these packs off, or you want me to do it?" She asked, watching the girls handle the work.

"I'll take what you got now, but after that, you handle all of it. I have to see for myself what the blocks are going to do at first anyway."

He stashed the work into the book bag as he and Truck hit the streets. He tried calling Hit-Man again but got no answer.

Where the fuck is this nigga at? He thought as they headed to Mobile to get it poppin'.

* * *

"Okay. Everybody know what to do, right?" Hit-Man said, looking in the back of the stolen van.

Everyone responded with a head nod except for P-Funk, who didn't like the fact that Hit-Man was trying to act like the boss.

Hit-Man just ignored him as he cocked the riot pump he was holding. A series of guns cocking followed as they all pulled their masks down over their faces.

"Let's do it," Vick said impatiently.

They all hopped out, running into the club. As soon as people saw the men rush in, they all got scared and put their hands in the air.

"Anybody move, they die," Hit-Man said as the six men surrounded the people at the bar and card games.

The men at the table looked at the group of masked men to see what they wanted.

Hit-Man walked up to the man sitting there like he was in charge and aimed the pump at his face. He demanded the money and drugs that he knew were there.

"Do you have any idea who you're robbing?" The man said, without an ounce of fear in his voice. "

You think I give a damn?" Hit-Man said as he smacked him with the butt of the gun. "Now shut the fuck up."

The man bent over, holding the back of his head. When he looked up at Hit-Man, he stared right into his eyes without even blinking and said, "You better sleep with one eye open, nigga!

That's not a threat either, so do what you got to," he said, knowing they were black from the way they talked.

Tired of listening to the man, P-Funk walked over and pushed Hit-Man out of the way. He gripped the man by the collar and picked him up out of the chair.

"Where is the stash at, old man, and you and everybody else get to walk up out of here."

"Fuck you!" The man replied.

P-Funk let him go and turned around like he was about to walk away. However, he spun back around so quickly that nobody saw it coming.

Boc!

One shot from the Calico tore into his kneecap and shattered the bone, separating the connecting joints. The pain the bullet inflicted made him obey their command. If he wasn't convinced before, he was now. These niggas weren't playing games.

"It's in the back room!" he screamed out in pain.

Vick and Trey searched through the back room vigorously until they found the money and work. It was nowhere near what they were expecting to find. After bagging everything up, they came back out with everything in hand.

"Let's get the fuck out of here," Vick announced, heading for the door.

The group of masked men started backing toward the door, never taking their eyes off of the men in the bar. Once everyone was in the van, P-Funk just had to do something extra. He turned around and let off numerous shots into the building, not caring if he hit anyone. He hopped into the van. They fled away from the scene thinking they were in the clear.

"What the fuck was that shit you just did? We were just supposed to grab the shit and get out," Hit-Man said angrily, mean-mugging P-Funk.

"I got answers, and because of it, this is what we got," P-Funk replied, pointing to the bag of dope and money. "He wasn't telling your bitch ass anything."

Hit-Man was tired of P-Funk disrespecting him every time his mouth opened. He wanted to put a bullet right through his skull. Feeling the tension in the air, Gunz tried to ease it up.

"So, how much you niggas think was in there?"

"It wasn't as much as we thought it would be, but they did have some gwap for us. I'm trying to figure out what kind of drugs this is, though," Vick said, digging into the bag and pulling out a package with the substance in it.

"We'll figure shit out when we get back to the crib. Put that up for now," Hit-Man said, looking at the missed calls on his phone.

He redialed Lit's number so he could talk to him. If they only knew what was about to come their way, they would have killed everybody in that place.

CHAPTER 10

Detective Eli sat at his desk looking over some pictures of a crime scene. It was puzzling to him because of what the witness said she saw. He knew she wasn't telling him everything she knew, but he didn't want to interrogate her too much yet. He was also waiting for his partner to get back with the video surveillance tapes from the store up the street where the murders took place.

As if on cue, Detective Washam walked right in and sat down across from him at her desk. She held up the DVD and had a smile on her face.

"Our witness has been lying to us about what she saw, and I got the proof right here."

"Talk to me," Eli said, giving her his full attention.

He was hoping that they were about to crack this case wide open.

"Well, not only does she know the shooters; she knows the male victim as well. The tape shows her and the female victim standing outside the bodega talking to the male. Her friend passed him what looks to be a house key, and he walks off in one direction, while they head back in the other direction," she said, pausing so Eli could take in what had she said so far.

"About half an hour later, the two girls returned to the same corner, but this time they hoped inside of a Dodge Charger with tinted windows. It doesn't show who was inside, but I'm willing to bet a hundred dollars that it's the killer or killers."

Detective Eli rubbed his beard as he listened to his partner. What they had was hopefully just enough to finally get the girl to tell them what really had happened in the house that night.

"So, what do you think? It was a robbery gone bad, and she and her friend had something to do with it?" Eli asked.

"Yep, but it went bad for them, because whoever they tried to rob was ready for the ambush," Detective Washam replied.

"Okay. Let's watch the DVD so I can hopefully catch something that you missed. Then, we're gonna go pay our witness another visit. This time, though, we won't be so nice," Eli said as they got up and headed to the video room.

"Uh oh. I know that look. What do you have up your sleeve, Earl?" she said to her partner, giving him a look of suspicion.

"I'll tell you all about it after we finish watching the video. I just have to make sure I'm not wrong on this first," he stated, closing the door behind them.

They sat in the video room and played the surveillance video over and over again for the next hour, trying to find something helpful to the case. Once they finished, they decided to talk to Kadeejah first thing in the morning. They headed home for the night.

* * *

It hadn't been a full two months yet, and already Lit and Hit-Man had made their mark in the streets as the new top dogs. There wasn't an ounce, quarter, half, or whole brick of heroin sold in Mobile, Birmingham, Montgomery, or Biloxi that they didn't have a part in. It was amazing to them, almost unbelievable. The amount of money they saw and drugs they sold in the past month and a half.

Being on top wasn't as easy as it seemed. There were more than enough problems that came along with the job. Workers were being busted and fucking up with money. Some claimed to be stuck up. You name it, it happened. It was definitely a hassle. In fact, it was a headache for them, but at the end of the day, it was all worth it. Whatever the case was, the streets were theirs now, or so they thought.

Hit-Man was still running around, recklessly robbing people, without Lit even knowing. He wanted it all, and nothing was going to stop him. Little did he know that Derrick and the others even robbed their people a couple of times but didn't say anything to Hit-Man. They kept the work and money for themselves.

Vick and Gunz had joined up with Lit and Hit-Man, and their blocks were back to doing numbers. Lit sold them a brick a week, and the money was coming in. As long as Lit dealt with Miguel and Quincy, he figured he would be a millionaire within the next year.

Chloe went from having just her three friends cutting, bagging, and stamping the dope to hiring six more women to help. They even expanded to a house on Northern Boulevard. Niggas thought she was sweet until she laid a couple of them down for trying her. They quickly realized that she was that bitch. Lit was proud that he put the right person in charge of the stash houses.

Lit and Hit-Man headed over to the house because he wanted to meet up with the top people. Even though Chloe wasn't a partner, he considered her one. Hit-Man had something that he needed to do, so he was hoping that it wouldn't take long. He had another meeting to be at with some people about some work he didn't know what to do with.

They pulled up to the crib, looking around and making sure nothing seemed out of place. They had to be that way because niggas would do anything to be in their positions. They would never catch them slipping, though.

They stepped out of the car and entered the building. When they walked into the apartment that was used as the conference room, twenty-two people were sitting around the table waiting. Chloe was one of them. Hit-Man and Lit stood at the head of the table so they could start the meeting.

"Okay, this is how it is. We have a sweet connect for the dope in Florida as well as in Mexico. They will get it to us in a timely fashion, and it's our job to get rid of it. The faster we can get rid of it, the faster we get more. I'm trying to lock up the East Coast. Chloe will take care of the distribution to all the North Mobile houses like she has been, and Hit-Man will handle Birmingham. I will handle Mobile. We have twenty-one houses now. That means the twenty-one of you sitting here are the heads of the households. Anything goes wrong, you need to call one of us immediately. Got it?" Lit said as everyone nodded.

"I just got us a few people on payroll from police stations in all our areas who will keep us in the loop on any investigations or random raids. It's pretty simple, so we all have to do our parts," Hit-Man explained as he rubbed his hands together.

Just as Lit was about to say something else, the front door opened. Everyone looked in that direction and stared at the figure standing before them. You would have thought they had seen a ghost. No one in their right mind expected to see this person, not even Lit or Hit-Man. He walked toward the table accompanied by the most beautiful woman they had ever seen. Even Chloe's pussy tingled at the sight of her.

At twenty-six years of age, Funchess was a bombshell. She stood 5'6, and her slender build gave her the look of a model, as did her facial features. Her neck was slim, long, and very delicate looking, and her shoulders dropped just right. Her face was oval and very much chiseled to perfection. Everything from her strapless Chanel dress to her three-inch stilettos screamed money. There was nobody fucking with her, and she knew it.

"What kind of operation are you running where people can just walk through the front door? Where is security? Better yet, why isn't anyone guarding the front door? Where are the shooters that should have been posted on the roof guarding your money?" He inquired with a calm yet attention-demanding voice.

No one could speak because they were still in awe of the man talking to them.

"What's wrong? Y'all act like y'all seen a ghost."

One of the young bulls at the table spoke up.

"I thought you were dead, sir. I went to your funeral with my mom," he explained as everyone else at the table nodded in agreement.

They all had been in their teens when they went to the biggest homecoming of a street legend. C.J.'s funeral was so packed that the police had to block off seven blocks all around the church. People from all over came to say their goodbyes to the person who was now standing before them.

"The funeral was an illusion to trick everybody and keep me safe from the feds as well as my enemies. It's amazing how many people looked into the casket but never checked to see if the person inside was breathing," C.J. stated. "I'm not here to talk about that right now, though. I'm here checking on my investment, and I'm not liking what I see. I want to speak with Lit, so everybody else get out."

They all looked from C.J. to Lit, but no one moved. C.J. removed his glasses from his face, and the murderous look in his eyes said it all.

"Now!" He yelled.

Everyone jumped up and headed out the door, never looking back. Funchess put her hand on his arm and whispered in his ear.

"I'll be outside in the car. Don't be too long, because we have to be on our jet to Mexico in two hours," she reminded him before giving him a kiss on the cheek and walking out the door so the men could talk.

As Hit-Man and Chloe headed outside, the whole block was surrounded by men dressed all in black, carrying assault rifles. That's when Hit-Man really realized how powerful his friend from prison truly was. He was a little mad that he only wanted to talk to Lit, but he didn't care, because he had to get somewhere important.

"What was that all about?" Chloe asked Hit-Man as they stood outside the door, staring at the men in black.

"I'm not even sure, but whatever happened, it made my homie come all the way from MIA to address it. I have to go handle something but tighten up security around here. Get a couple of shooters up on each roof so nothing like this will happen again," Hit-Man said as he headed for his car.

"What if Lit needs to talk to you?" Chloe said, watching Funchess walk to the awaiting car parked in the middle of the street.

"Tell him to hit my phone. I'll be back in a couple of hours to check on you," he stated before hopping into the car and pulling off.

* * *

"So what brings you all the way out here?" Lit asked, giving C.J. a half hug.

"I came to pick up my wife's cousin. She missed her, so you know how that is. I could have easily put her ass on a plane, but I also wanted to check on Quincy and Miguel. I see that business is booming right now," he said, sitting on the edge of the table.

"Yeah. We have a lot of area on lock right now. I'm trying to have this shit the way you had it," Lit said.

"No. I want you to just do you, and you will prosper in this game."

"So why did you need to talk to me alone?"

C.J. stood up and paced back and forth around the room a couple of times before stepping in front of Lit.

"I want you to take a good look at your inner circle and make sure that everyone is in their right spot on your team. Hit-Man's supposed to be your partner, but there's something about him that's not adding up. You can tell a man's heart by his eyes. The eyes never lie, Lit. That is why I'm only dealing with you. Just be careful with the company you keep."

Lit listened to C.J. talk for a while. He thought about what he had told him, because it was the second time someone had said that to him. This time, though, he would be hands-on with everything going on.

"Thanks for coming, though, and I'm going to tighten up on things to make sure this operation is running smooth," Lit stated.

"Well, let me get out of here. If you need to speak with me, just let Miguel or Quincy know, and either one of them will be able to contact me. I can't keep the misses waiting too long." He smirked, shaking Lit's hand.

Lit watched as C.J. left the building. C.J.' s henchmen waited until he was safely in the SUV before they dispersed into one of the six other SUVs. The fleet of cars pulled out into traffic like they owned the city. Lit knew he would be that way one day, and he smiled at his homie.

CHAPTER 11

Over the next couple of weeks, Big Eazy laid low, letting the healing process of his body take place. Every day he talked to Blimp, who kept his ears in the streets to see if he heard anything yet, but still no luck. He was starting to get impatient, because the longer he sat around, the longer he wouldn't make any money. It was time to start getting some answers to the questions he had on his mind.

He strapped on his shoulder holster along with his twin Glocks, after putting on his bulletproof vest. He slid the extra clips in place. He walked over to the mirror to check himself out. Big Eazy had on all black, with a skully cap to match. After being satisfied with his appearance, he went downstairs to wait for Blimp, who was on his way over to pick him up.

***

"What's up with you? You ready to go put in some work?" Blimp asked when Big Eazy got into the car.

"I was born ready. Now, let's go find out where my shit at," Big Eazy replied as he leaned back in the seat.

"This dude's mom who I know from the Southeast asked me if I had put out some work there, because she's seen the bags with the same stamp that we use, about two weeks ago when she copped something. When I asked her where, she said over on Creekside Avenue, so I think we should start there," Blimp stated.

"The dumb muthafuckas didn't even change the bags. How stupid can they be? Let's head over there and pay these niggas a little visit," Big Eazy said, puffing on some loud. "They should have never taken my shit."

* * *

"What you need, Double A?" Lil Renard asked as the fiend walked over toward the group of boys.

"Let me get two Bs," Double A replied, holding up the money for them.

"Give me the dough and walk over to my man. He will take care of you," Lil Renard stated. "I need some more of that loud that Vick gave us that time. That shit was fire."

"I know, man. I haven't had anything like that in a minute. When he comes to pick this money up, I'ma ask him where I can get some more of it all," Bricks said.

"Yeah, I can smoke half a Dutch and be lit off that shit. We definitely need that. I'll pay him for a GP of it."

"Me too. We can grab that and blow it with these two freaks out north this weekend. They both keep blowing up my phone trying to hook up again. I told them MOB."

"Money over bitches," they both said in unison.

"Yo! Who that cruising through the block like that?" Renard asked, watching the Ford Taurus slow down a little.

The windows were tinted, so they couldn't see inside.

"It's probably the pigs. I'm glad we don't have anything on us right now. You sold the last joints you had, right?" Bricks asked.

"Yeah. That's why I told bull to get it from you. I'm about to get the rest out of the crib when these muthafuckas leave and stop harassing us."

The car kept going, not even paying them any attention. They watched it turn the corner, and they smiled at each other. There were a few people outside. They thought that the cops didn't feel like hearing the people's mouths.

"They must have thought we were going to run or something. We sure showed their asses," Bricks said, with a laugh.

* * *

"Why didn't you stop? That's them pussies right there," Big Eazy said impatiently.

"Man, it's too many people outside right now, bro. We can wait and come back later to get them," Blimp replied.

"Fuck those people. Go back around the block, nigga! We gonna set an example out of this bitch. Nobody takes my shit and thinks I'm just gonna let it slide. I bet no one will disrespect us again. I'm going to get some answers right now, even if I have to expose these bitch ass niggas in front of everybody. Now, stop right in front of them!" Big Eazy demanded.

Thinking erratically, Big Eazy jumped out of the car, with his hand gripping the Glock that he pulled out from its holster. The move he made was so sudden that it caught everyone on the block by surprise.

"Listen up," he began as he waved the gun aimlessly at the crowd of people, who were scrambling to get out of the way. "I want every last one of you lil niggas to pay attention 'cause I'm dead fucking serious!"

Big Eazy spoke to no one in particular because he didn't know who knew something about his shit, but he still continued to yell at the niggas, who were left frozen in their tracks.

Bricks and Renard stood there stuck, wishing they had gone inside the house like they had started. They didn't even have their guns, which were hiding under the front tires of their cars parked in front of the door. When Big Eazy walked over toward them and singled them out, they knew something was about to happen.

"You two bitch ass niggas, come the fuck over here. I believe y'all have or had something that belongs to me, and I want it back. I also want to know who gave it to you!" He said, not wanting to play games.

"Nigga, we don't know what the fuck you talking about. Miss me with that shit you talking," Renard stated, not backing down from the two men holding the guns on them.

When Renard puffed out his chest like he wanted to fight or something, Big Eazy lifted the Glock and aimed it at his leg.

Boc! Boc!

The gun sounded, and Renard screamed like a bitch getting beaten the fuck up.

"Shut your bitch ass up, nigga, before the next shot rocks your ass to sleep!" He snapped.

The people from the block watching were scared to death and didn't know what to do. Renard held his leg, while Bricks stood there motionless.

"I want to know who came up with the bright idea to rob me and try to kill me?" He said, looking over at Bricks for an answer.

"Like my man said, we don't know what the fuck you're talking about. We got our work from my man, and even if I did know, I wouldn't tell you shit. I'm no snitch, muthafucka!" Bricks yelled back.

Big Eazy liked the young bull's heart, but right now he wasn't trying to hear any of that. He walked up to Bricks and smacked him in the head with his gun.

"Both of you get in the trunk right now before you don't see tomorrow." When neither of them moved, Blimp took over and shot Renard in his other knee.

Boc!

"Okay, okay, nigga! Don't shoot him again," Bricks yelled out, feeling sorry for his friend.

Blimp popped open the trunk of the car, and Bricks helped his homie over to the car. He hoped that someone had called the police and informed them of the shots. He didn't like the cops, but they were the only ones who might be able to save them right now. Once they both were in the trunk, Blimp got in the driver's seat, while Rigs addressed the crowd of onlookers that was still left.

"If I find out any of you called the cops, that will be you taking that ride next," Big Eazy said as he hopped in the car and Blimp sped off.

A few minutes later, cops were everywhere trying to figure out what was going on.

* * *

They had the two young boys tied up in an abandoned building by a junkyard on 61st and Pike Avenue. Since all the junkyards were closed, they weren't worried about anyone hearing them. Big Eazy stood over Renard, who was still in so much pain.

"I see you're not talking all that shit now, are you?" Big Eazy smirked. "I just want to know where my work and money are, and I'll let you walk. I mean crawl, up outta here."

Renard looked up, ice-grilling Big Eazy and Blimp. If looks could kill, they both would have been dead. Big Eazy walked over to Bricks, who until now hadn't been touched.

"Are you gonna tell us what we need to know, or do you want the same thing we gave your friend over there?"

"Fuck you! I'm not telling you shit!" Bricks exclaimed before spitting in Big Eazy's face.

Big Eazy wiped his face with the bottom part of his shirt. He nodded over to Blimp, who had a bat resting on his shoulder. Blimp smiled and walked up to Bricks and started swinging wildly at his body. He continuously hit him with the wooden bat. Bricks caught a barrage of painful blows, mostly to his arms and legs. Once he became tired of swinging the bat, Blimp began punching Bricks repeatedly in the face.

Bricks was covered in blood by the time Blimp took a break from the vicious attack. There was an enormous amount of pain shooting throughout his entire body. He laughed maniacally to further infuriate them. Big Eazy and Blimp beat Bricks over and over again for twenty minutes straight. They were violent and callous in their attempt to get answers, but he held water. Anyone else in his situation would have broken, but not Bricks. Unhappy about his obvious lack of willingness to cooperate, Big Eazy shot him in the head at point-blank range.

Renard was struggling to get free, when he saw his man take a bullet to the head. He knew he had to do something if he wanted to get out of this alive. They approached him, ready to end his life as well, when he nodded in defeat.

Blimp removed the duct tape from Renard's mouth.

"You want to tell us something?" He questioned.

"I'll tell you where we got the work from. Just, please, don't kill me," Renard said, defeated.

"Who gave it to you?" Big Eazy asked in a calm voice.

Renard started telling everything he knew in an attempt to live. He really didn't know anything, but he gave them all types of information, like he was talking to the cops. If he only knew how close to the truth he really was, he might have said something earlier. Big Eazy and Blimp listened to Renard talk, with anger all over their faces. Big Eazy couldn't believe the name that came out of his mouth.

After they got what they needed from Renard, Blimp silenced him forever with two shots to the heart. Usually, he would have given him a wig shot, but because he told them what they needed to know. They let his family be able to give him an open-casket funeral instead of a closed one. They left the two bodies there to be found by whoever opened the building in the morning, as they headed back home to prepare for war.

* * *

When Hit-Man realized that some of the drugs they took were crystal meth, he didn't know what to do with it right away. He called one of his white boys, who lived in a small town in Alabama, called Bay-Minette.

Brandon knew a lot about meth because he used to sell, use, cook, and distribute it. He told Hit-Man to meet him at his crib in an hour and they would discuss it then.

Hit-Man started heading in that direction so he could get back before Lit came through. They were going to the club that night to celebrate their success in the game.

He parked in front of Brandon's crib just as Brandon was parking. They greeted one another and then headed inside.

"So, show me what you got," Brandon stated, looking down at the gym bag that Hit-Man was carrying.

Hit-Man passed Brandon the bag, and Brandon sat it on the table. When he opened it, he knew what it was just by looking at it. He motioned for Hit-Man to take a seat so he could explain everything and put him up on game.

"A lot of people don't make meth the right way. See, after they do the whole process with the lithium, cold pack, sulfuric acid, Sudafed, etc., they skip an entire process. Really, all they are making is bathtub crank, and they wash it down with acetone and call it Ice. Fucking lame! They have a couple of people tweaking because of that shit. Real Ice like you just showed me right there is easy to come by if you know the right people. I know people who will take that off your hands ASAP if you're trying to sell it wholesale," Brandon said.

"I'm still trying to figure out what I'm going to do with it," Hit-Man replied.

All kinds of thoughts were going through his head now. He wanted that fast money.

"Well, if you don't want to sell it like that, you can do it this way and still come up. Break it down to quarters, but instead of the .25, make them .18 so you'll have six quarters instead of four. Sell each one at $50, so that's $300 a gram at 1,000 grams. I think you can figure that out." He smirked. Hit-Man was doing the numbers in his head while listening. "So, as you can see, there's a lot you can do."

"I don't want to hold it too long, so just see if you can get rid of it for a good price, and I'll break you off. I'm gonna leave it here with you, but don't try and play me," Hit-Man warned him.

"You know I'm not like that."

"I'm just saying. Anyway, I have to go get ready 'cause me and my homie are hitting the club tonight. Just hit my cell when you're ready for me."

They shook hands and Hit-Man left. He was about to make a hefty profit off of somebody else's work. He still had to split it with Vick and them, but it was all free money, so he didn't care.

CHAPTER 12

Lit and Hit-Man had moved up in the game fast as hell. To stroke their egos, they copped whips. Lit bought a 2022 Denali with televisions in the headrests, front visors, and even one in the steering wheel. He had Lambo doors on the front that lifted up, and rear doors that opened like those on a Maybach.

Hit-Man kept it simple with a 2022 Lexus GS. It had a system so loud that you could hear it a mile away. Literally! The platinum rims blinded people when the sun was out. The leather seats warmed up in the winter and cooled down in the summer. It was candy apple red with wooden interior.

Lit's Denali was black on black. They both had two percent tint on their windows, making it impossible to see who was inside. The two vehicles came as a gift, courtesy of Miguel, who liked the way they were moving his product. He had hooked Lit and Hit-Man up with his cousin who owned a dealership, and he gave them a great deal on the vehicles.

They followed each other down the block, and all eyes were on their cars. They pulled up in front of Curtis Place, stuntin' on all the watchful eyes. As they stepped out of the cars, all the ladies stared and tried to figure out who the two men were. They were hoping to be the chosen ones who would get to leave with them that night. Even the niggas had to admit that Hit-Man and Lit looked and smelled like money. Lit walked to the front of the line and discretely handed the bouncer one hundred dollars as he shook his hand. He let the two men in as the rest of the people in the line stood there ice-grilling them.

"Let these ten ladies come with us," Hit-Man stated, giving him two more C-notes. He smirked at the group of haters, giving them something else to hate on, before heading inside with his entourage of women right behind him.

Lit stayed on the floor instead of going over to the VIP section. He needed to mingle with the ordinary people for a while, so that he didn't forget where he came from. He grabbed two stacks in ones and went over to the stage. The dancer was killing the pole. She rode it like she was riding a dick. Lit started throwing the ones at her when she climbed to the top and then twerked as she slowly slid down it.

"Why you not in VIP with everybody else?" Chloe asked, walking up beside him.

"I'm having more fun down here with my peoples than up there. Feel me?" he said, swinging his arm around.

"That's what's up!" she said, tossing ones at the dancer. "This shit is packed tonight!"

"Yeah, it's wet panties night. You should get up there and show these bitches up!" He yelled over the music.

Chloe smiled at him, giving him a playful shove. As the dancer leaned down, Chloe placed a bunch of ones in her G-string.

"I'd put these bitches to shame!" She smirked.

Lit laughed as they both headed over to the table where Hit-Man was sitting.

"Assalamu 'alaikum," Amir said as Lit greeted him with a half hug.

"Wa alaikum salaam wa rahmatu-lah wa barakatu," Lit replied, sitting down. "I didn't know you were coming here tonight."

"I brought one of my homies out here. When I saw Hit-Man, I knew your ass was here," he joked.

He looked over at Chloe and said, "You looking sexy as hell, lil cousin."

"A bitch like me is always fly. Just because I like pussy don't mean I can't still keep niggas' mouths drooling."

She gave him a hug, and everyone sat down in the booth to enjoy themselves. Strippers were dancing around them, and they were tipping all of them. The vibe was relaxing until a couple of girls walked up to Chloe.

"Excuse me but was you at Incahutes a couple of weeks ago?" A dark-skinned girl with a long weave asked.

"Yeah, why? What's up?"

"You got my man jumped, and now he has a broken jaw because of you. If I didn't have this dress on right now, I would beat that ass. I will be seeing you soon, bitch! Believe me," she stated as she walked away.

The girl's two friends rolled their eyes and followed her.

Chloe sat there with a smile on her face. She wanted to grab the bottle she had on the table and smash it into the girl's face and give her a broken jaw to match her dude's but Lit held her arm.

"This is not the right place, ma. Let's enjoy ourselves, and we'll catch her and that nigga later."

"I'm cool! I have to use the bathroom real quick," she said, getting up and heading toward the ladies' room.

As she moved through the crowd, she could see the girl who had just approached her walk into the ladies' room ahead of her. She looked around to see where her friends were. She spotted them flirting with some niggas as they watched them shooting water guns onstage at the dancers. Chloe suddenly felt a rush shoot through her body as she realized this was her opportunity to catch the girl slipping.

When Chloe reached the bathroom door, she removed her gun from under her dress and stuck it in her purse. She then removed a pair of brass knuckles and slipped her fingers through the loops as she quietly pushed open the door. Three ladies were walking out, leaving just the two of them in the bathroom. The girl was in one of the stalls. Chloe set her purse down on the sink counter and waited for her to come out.

The toilet flushed, and the moment the girl stepped out of the stall, Chloe hit her dead in the throat, causing her to bend over in pain.

"What was that shit you were talking now?" Chloe asked as the girl fell backward, holding her throat. "You're not with your friends now, bitch! Talk that shit to me now!"

The girl was gasping for air, when Chloe kicked her in the stomach, ramming her heel into her ribs. She pulled her over to one of the stalls and slammed her head into the toilet.

"I don't know who the fuck you thought I was, but you should have done your homework, muthafucka!" she said, pulling her head out of the toilet. "You lucky I'm in a good mood; otherwise, yo ass would be leaving here in a body bag."

Chloe smashed her head on the toilet again. This time leaving the badly beaten woman there in a bloody mess and still gasping for air. Before walking away, Chloe spit on her and kicked her again in the ribs.

"Dumb ass bitch," Chloe said, flushing the toilet.

She checked herself in the mirror and walked back out to the party. When she sat down, Lit stared at her momentarily before he puffed on the loud he was smoking. "You good?" he asked.

Chloe leaned over and whispered in his ear, "All this shit that just happened has a bitch horny!" Her pussy was soaking wet from the adrenaline rush she just had.

"What happened?" he asked, feeling his dick hardening inside his jeans.

"I just beat that bitch's ass in the bathroom, so I think we need to get the hell outta here."

A woman's scream caused everyone to look in the direction of the sound. The girl staggered out of the bathroom with blood all over her clothes. People started shouting and running toward the door, trying to get out of there before the authorities arrived. Bouncers rushed over to her to see what had happened.

"Come on! Let's bounce," Lit said as he got up.

"Where y'all going?" Gerald asked.

"Your cousin just put in some work. I'm going to take her home. Hit me up tomorrow if you want to do something. Hit-Man, I'm outta here! Make sure you handle that shit for me too."

"Cool. I'm about to grab a couple of these bitches to take home with me. I might as well enjoy this money you're leaving!" Hit-Man exclaimed, holding up the stacks of money.

Lit and Chloe headed out the back of the club toward his car. The cops were just pulling up as they turned out of the parking lot.

"Where did you park?" He asked.

"My friend Peaches has my whip. Let's stop at her crib so I can get it."

Lit stopped at the light just as a car pulled up beside them. Its passenger side window came down, and he could see the barrel of a pump aimed at him and Chloe. He hit the gas pedal just as the first shot went off.

Boom!

The car took off behind them, trying to catch up.

"Who the fuck is that?" Lit yelled out.

Chloe pulled out her 9 mm from her purse and started busting back at the car chasing them.

Boc! Boc! Boc! Boc! Boc!

"Drive this muthafucka, nigga!"

She kept firing at the car until she saw it swerve out of control and hit a parked car. Lit sped off all the way to Peaches house, where he parked his truck in the back of her crib.

Chloe had already called her and told her they were coming, so the back door was already open. They went inside and locked the door behind them.

"Who the fuck just tried to kill us?" Lit asked.

"I don't know. But that shit really got my pussy wet. Peaches! Bring your ass down here!" Chloe ordered.

"Listen to your freak ass," Lit said, shaking his head at her. "Niggas tried to get at us, and all you thinking about is busting a nut?"

Chloe gave him the middle finger as Peaches came downstairs wearing a pair of boy shorts and a wifebeater. She walked over and sat down on Chloe's lap, giving her a kiss. Chloe played with her nipples, making Peaches let out a soft moan.

"You know what I need right now, so handle your business," she said, opening up her legs for both Lit and Peaches to see.

Peaches got on her knees between Chloe's legs and pulled off her thong. She could see Chloe's juices already leaking from her vagina. Peaches started slurping it up as she stuck her tongue out and began playing with her clit. Chloe leaned her head back and closed her eyes.

"Damn! Y'all seriously going to do this shit right now in front of me?" Lit asked, watching them put on a show.

He couldn't take his eyes off of Peaches ass that was poking out of her boy shorts.

When they didn't respond, he got up and walked behind Peaches. He squeezed her ass, feeling its softness. Lit then pulled down her shorts and stuck two fingers into her pussy.

"Mmmm!" Peaches moaned.

"That's right, nigga! Get your shit off! That's my bitch, so you can get it in with us," Chloe replied.

He strapped on a condom and entered Peaches from behind. She started throwing her ass back onto Lit as he gripped her waist to keep his balance. Chloe felt herself about to cum and started moving her hips in circles on Peaches tongue.

"Oh, ma. Suck this shit!" Chloe screamed as she squirted all into Peaches mouth. Peaches continued sucking on Chloe's clit until she busted another nut.

The two girls switched positions, and so did Lit. He lay down, and Chloe straddled his dick. Peaches knelt on the couch with her ass up in the air in Chloe's face. Chloe started fingering Peaches ass and pussy simultaneously, which drove Peaches crazy. She started biting down on the pillow. Chloe started moving her tongue in and out of Peaches asshole like a snake. Lit kept lifting Chloe up and down on his shaft. He felt himself about to cum and slowed down because he didn't want to cum too fast.

Chloe felt his dick swelling up, so she grabbed it with her pussy muscles and started working her hips. Lit couldn't take it any longer and pulled out just in time to explode all over her back. Peaches came a couple minutes later into Chloe's mouth. The three of them went upstairs to Peaches room to finish what they had started.

CHAPTER 13

"How many you need?" Aaron asked the fiend as she walked over to the porch. Vick and Gunz were sitting in the car talking to him.

She turned around to see who said it was. Her eyes then got big, and a smile came across her face. She strutted over to where Aaron was sitting. "I was looking for you, Aaron. Can I get a bundle until I get paid on Friday?"

"Fuck no! You can't get anything from me until you give me the money you already owe me!" Aaron blurted out.

"Come on, Aaron. You know you're going to get your money. You can take me to the ATM. Please. I'm feeling bad right now," she begged while licking her lips.

Aaron looked at the woman standing before him, with anger on his face. Even though she was on dope, she kept herself clean and put together. She had on a pair of black tights and a long shirt that came down just over her ass. Her hair was in a wrap, and she had on a pair of Jordans that Aaron had bought her for her birthday.

"I said no. Now take your ass home and get away from this block. No money, no dope," he said, waving her away.

"Who the hell are you talking to like that? I brought you into this world, and I'll take you out."

Both Gunz and Vick looked at each other and then back at Aaron and the woman. Aaron was talking to his mother like she was a piece of shit. Gunz stepped out of the car just as Aaron smacked her.

"Yo. Why are you putting your hands on your mom? I don't give a fuck what she does out here, but you better not ever let me see you do that again," Gunz said, helping her off the ground.

"That's crazy, bro!" Vick shouted as he hopped out of the car. "That's your mom, nigga! Show her some respect."

"You okay, miss?" Gunz asked.

"Yes, I'm not like this all the time. I know how to control my addiction, but I just needed a lil something to get me through the day."

"Where do you live at?"

"I live on Dauphin Street. Why are you asking me that?" she said, looking at Gunz.

"Come on! I'll drop you off and give you something to hold you over, but I want my money on Friday."

"Thank you so much, and I get my check after twelve o'clock, so you can pick it up whenever."

"Yo, I'ma drop his mom off real quick and grab something to eat from Church's. You rolling?"

"Nah! I'm going to count this money until you get back," Vick stated, already knowing what his friend was about to do.

Gunz pulled off with Aaron's mom in the passenger seat. He kept peeking over between her legs, looking at her pussy lips poking through her tights. She caught his glances and smiled to herself. She opened and shut her legs a couple of times before Gunz stopped in front of her door. He then pulled out two bundles and passed them to her.

"Let me thank you for this," she said, placing her hand on his lap. "I can tell that you was thinking the same thing."

She began rubbing on the crotch of his pants, bringing his man to attention. She unzipped them, pulled out his dick, and then inserted it into her mouth. Her warm lips made Gunz close his eyes and lean his head back.

"Damn, girl. Your head game is on point," he stated, holding the back of her head.

He stuck his hand inside the back of her tights and made his way from her ass to her pussy. She was already wet. He stuck his finger into her hole and started fingering her pussy. Seconds later, Gunz busted his load into her mouth.

"Why don't you come inside for a few minutes? I can make you feel so much better," she said, sucking her juices off of his fingers.

"I already got what I wanted right now. I'll get at you some other time. I have to get back to my money right now," he replied, fixing his pants.

She stepped out of the car, closing the door behind her as Gunz sped off.

He headed back over to Raven Drive to pick his man back up. He laughed at the fact that he just received a blowjob from one of his worker's moms. However, his smile quickly faded when he thought about the fact that she was strung out on dope, and he hadn't used a condom.

He pulled up to the crib and parked. When he got out of the car, Vick and Aaron were walking out. Vick had a book bag of money in his hand.

"You ready, nigga?" Vick asked.

"Yeah. Let's slide over to West End and check on the other spot real quick before we shoot out to Birmingham," Gunz suggested, getting back into the car.

"Soon as I get another bag for y'all, I'll hit your jack, big homie," Aaron stated.

"Alright, cannon," Vick replied.

They pulled out of the parking spot just as Vick noticed a cop car coming up the wrong way. Gunz also noticed it, and he was about to back out the other way, but an unmarked car was heading up the block. Something was about to go down, and they were right in the middle of it.

"Yo! Put the straps up. We don't want to get caught with the money and guns," Gunz said, removing his weapon from his waist.

"Fuck that, nigga. We got work in here too, remember?" Vick blurted out. "Damn. We can't even run!"

"Let's just see what these pigs want with us. If they get out of line, we riding the fuck out. Tuck the straps under the seat for now. Just leave them close enough to reach for if we need to," Gunz said.

Two detectives exited their cars and walked up to Gunz and Vick. Gunz rolled down the driver's window as they approached. "What can we do for you officers?" He asked.

"First off, you can shut off the engine and step out of the car," Detective Eli said, pointing his gun at them.

Detective Washam and six other officers had their guns aimed at them as well.

For the first time, Vick and Gunz noticed that there were more than just two police cars.

"What did we do?" Vick asked, stepping out of the car with his hands up. It would have been a death wish if he and Gunz had tried shooting it out with them.

Even though they had guns, drugs, and money in the car, they knew they would be able to make bail. It was only twenty bundles, which they had in the stash box. But it was the money and guns that would be found.

The guns were registered to Gunz's brother, who never had been arrested before, and the car was in his name as well, so they could say they didn't know the guns were there. Gunz had already texted his brother with a code word to let him know.

After frisking the two men and cuffing them, Washam read them their Miranda rights.

Eli had a big smile on his face, and Vick and Gunz were wondering why he was looking at them like that.

"What's so funny, pig, and why we being detained?" Vick inquired.

"Let's just say you two have been some bad young men. Do you know a young lady named Kadeejah?" Eli asked. "Before you answer that question, remember that what you say can be held against you in a court of law."

"Fuck you! And we don't know that bitch," Vick said angrily.

"Well, it seems that she knows you, and she had some very interesting things to say about the night her friend and her brother were killed. Guess who was holding the smoking gun? Bingo," Washam said with a grin, pointing a finger at the both of them.

Both Gunz and Vick wanted to kick themselves for leaving the bitch alive. They knew the code of the streets was never to leave a witness who could point you out. Now they were most likely looking at murder charges. One positive was that the two detectives were so happy they had caught them that they didn't check the car, so they didn't find the guns and money. Vick and Gunz hoped like hell they could get out of this.

* * *

Lit was awakened by the sound of his phone ringing. He sat up in bed and then looked at the screen. He didn't recognize the phone number, so he silenced the rings. He got up and headed toward the bathroom when it started ringing again. This time he decided to answer the call.

"Hello?" he said, irritated. "Who is this?"

"Lit, last night some niggas came through the block on some gangsta shit and shot Renard and Bricks," the young bull said.

"Where they at now?" Lit asked while taking a piss.

"I don't know. They put them in the trunk of their car and peeled off. Nobody has seen them since."

"Did you call Hit-Man?"

"I tried his phone ten times and got no answer. That's why I called you. What do you want me to do?"

Lit went back into the bedroom. He thought about the night he had just had with Chloe and Peaches, and his dick started swelling up again. "Keep trying Hit-Man's number, and I'll also try. Did they take anything?" Lit asked while putting on his clothes.

"Not that we know of," the young boy replied.

"I'm in Maysville now. I'll be there in about an hour. Round up some niggas and let them know to strap up and be ready to move as soon as I get there," Lit said as he ended the phone call.

Chloe heard the conversation and was already out of bed and getting dressed. She threw on some black tights, a wifebeater, black Timberlands, and a black hoodie. She loved to get it poppin,' and the thought of getting ready to bust her gun had her pussy creaming up. She removed the two chrome 380s from the dresser drawer and checked the clips to make sure they were fully loaded. She threw on the shoulder holster and placed the guns inside.

"I'm ready whenever you are," she told Lit, grabbing her skully and bulletproof vest.

"Let's roll, then. Niggas just grabbed a couple of my coworkers, and we need to find out what the fuck is going on. Muthafuckas have to learn the hard way not to fuck with me," he replied, cocking his hammer, and then tucking it in his waistline. They headed out the door, ready to lay down anybody who had something to do with it.

CHAPTER 14

"Uggghh!" Champ snapped, flipping over the table. Food, fruit, and drinks went flying everywhere.

It had been a few days since his club had been robbed, and no one had yet brought him any information about the culprits who did it. Frustration was building all over his face, and everyone around him was beginning to notice it. Champ stared out the window of his plush office.

While everyone started picking up the things that fell on the floor, one of Champ's street workers walked in and closed the door behind him. He had his phone to his ear, talking to someone on the other line.

"Wait a sec. I want you to tell him everything you just told me, "He said as he passed the phone over to Champ.

Champ put the phone to his ear to talk to the caller. After listening to what he had to say, his face turned beet red. You could see the steam coming from his ears. He passed the phone back to his worker and walked over to his desk. Once he sat down, he looked up.

"Send some men over there and bring him to me alive. Everybody else around him, you know what to do," Champ stated, lighting up a cigar.

"Got it," the man said as he exited the office. He looked at the people sitting around waiting for his command. They were all killers anxiously ready to put in work for their boss.

"Load up. We got work to do," Angel said as he walked over and opened up the artillery room.

Everyone grabbed assault rifles and headed toward the four vans parked outside. None of the men said a word the whole time. They sat quietly with venom in their eyes.

"Where are we going, boss?" The driver asked, pulling out into traffic as the three other vans followed.

"Head over to West Maysville. We are about to pull a snatch and grab. These muthafuckas don't know who they are dealing with.

It's time to show these putas that nobody takes anything from the cartel," Angel stated as he pulled on a pair of black gloves.

The caravan got off the exit on Azalea Road and headed toward Village Green Drive. The hit squad started checking the magazines in their weapons and taking off the safeties as they approached their target. Angel spotted the person he was coming for getting into a car and then pulling off. "Follow that car right there."

The car was heading toward University Boulevard. Once they got to 15th and 3rd, stopping at a red light, Angel and his team made their move. The first van swerved around the car and cut in front of it, blocking it from trying to pull off. The second van blocked it from behind while the other two vans pulled up on the side of it. Angel noticed that there was more than just the one person he was looking for inside, and he knew what was about to pop off.

The van doors opened, and the assault team hopped out with their weapons aimed, and ready for war. The driver of the car stepped on the gas pedal, and the car lunged forward into the van. The car rammed into one of the men as all hell broke loose.

The occupants of the car were far outnumbered and outgunned. The assault team's guns lit up the sky like the Fourth of July. Angel's gun was spitting out bullets like everyone else's, and in the moment, he wasn't even thinking about what his boss had told him. Although they got off a couple of rounds at Angel and his crew, all the men in the car were annihilated.

The sounds of cop cars approaching caused them to cease fire on the car and turn their weapons on the police. As the fleet of police cars came into view, the killers let their weapons sing another song. Bullets riddled the cop cars and their occupants inside.

"Let's move!" Angel ordered as he jumped into the van.

They peeled out of there before more cops converged on them, leaving what would be known as one of the biggest massacres in the history of Alabama. Over ten officers were slaughtered, along with the four people in the car.

Angel rode in silence, as he had to figure out what he was going to tell his boss when they returned. Nothing went as expected, and the end result was that the person they went to snatch was now dead.

* * *

Lit and Chloe arrived at the DJ house to find twenty men waiting for them, all dressed in black. They looked around the room searching for Hit-Man, but he still wasn't there. He hadn't answered his phone all day. Lit walked over to where his young lieutenant was standing and shook his hand.

"You ready to put in some work, cannon?"

"I was born ready," he replied, cocking his burner and tucking it back in his waist.

"Okay, lil nigga. I hear you. Has anybody heard anything from Hit-Man? Something is definitely not right, and we need to find him," Lit said. His phone began ringing, and he grabbed it from his pocket.

"We haven't seen Hit-Man since the club. He hasn't even been here to pick up no money or anything," the bull replied.

"Let me take this call, and I'll get back to you in a few minutes," Lit said while walking away to answer the call.

Chloe followed him into the kitchen.

"This is a free call from an inmate in the Alabama prison system," the operator announced.

Lit waited for the operator to finish, and he then pressed one to accept the call.

"What's good with you, Vick?" he asked, placing the phone on speaker so Chloe could hear.

"Yo, Me and Gunz got pinched on a murder charge because of some bitch. We at the Metro on St. Emmanuel. I tried to hit Hit-Man up, but he's not answering. Can you get us a lawyer to get us up out of here?" Vick asked.

"Yeah. We've been trying his jack too, but with no response. I'm going to send someone over to munch with some cash to try and find out what's going on."

"Thanks, man. This shit has been fucked up ever since we hit that club and took that work. That nigga really been acting funny," Vick said.

"Yo! Watch what you're saying on here, and what the fuck you mean? Whose spot did y'all hit?" Lit asked, not taking heed of what he had just told his man not to do.

"These cartel niggas. Hit-Man asked us to help him out, and we would split the proceeds. I thought you knew about that shit," Vick replied.

"I didn't know anything about that, but let me get off this phone, man. You never know who's listening to our calls. If you don't hear from the lawyer in two days, hit me back up."

"Alright. Be safe out there."

Lit ended the call and then looked over to Chloe with a surprised look on his face. She must have been thinking the same thing because her expression said it all.

"Do you think that's what this shit is all over? He's been out there robbing people and didn't even put us up on game?" She asked in disbelief.

"I don't know, but I'm not gonna let nothing come in between my money, and I'm definitely not going to let my man get murked by these clown ass niggas. So if they want to go to war, then that's what we're going to do."

"That's all it is then. If you're riding, then so am I. What do you want to do about this?" Chloe asked.

"It's time to make our presence known in these streets again. So let's start by laying down a couple of niggas. I know I'm gonna die soon being out here. When death do come for me, though, it's going to have to catch me because I'm not sitting around waiting for it," Lit said, trying to drop some deep words on Chloe.

"Let's get it popping, then."

"Let me call my man real quick 'cause we can use his help on this. He's one of the niggas I know is about that life, and he'll have my back," Lit said, dialing Truck's number.

After talking with Truck, Lit and Chloe gathered up their crew, hopped in about eight different cars, and then headed out to handle business.

* * *

Angel and his crew rode around the city wreaking havoc on every spot they saw, hoping to draw out the man who was behind taking their work. Blood was being shed, and it didn't matter if it belonged to the cops or the thugs. Everybody was getting it.

They pulled up in front of another drug spot that his informant told him about, and they watched the traffic going in and out. The spot looked like it was making a lot of money with all the activity that was taking place.

"Let's move!" Angel announced, stepping out of the van.

His men scrambled out of the vehicles on his orders, and in one swift motion, they rushed the house and shot everyone moving except a man and his fourteen-year-old son who were now being held at gunpoint.

Angel walked into the house where they were, and looked over at the man, who was looking very nervous at the moment.

"I found these two counting money in the other room, so I figured they may know something about your shit," Angel's right-hand man stated.

"Cual de ustedes cabrones robaron mi mierda? (Which one of you bastards stole my shit?)" Angel asked the man in Spanish, noticing that he was Puerto Rican.

"I don't know what you are talking about! I haven't taken anything from anyone, and I damn sure don't know who did," he replied confidently.

"So, you do speak English, huh? Well maybe this will refresh your mind."

Angel pulled out his burner, raised his arm, and shot the man's son in the back of the head. The silencer that he had slipped on before entering the house had muffled the sound, but it did nothing to limit the damage. Blood and skull sprayed out of the boy's head, and he crashed to the floor on his face. Angel pumped two more shots into the boy as he then stepped over his body.

"Why you kill my son? He had nothing to do with any of this!" The man screamed out, looking at his son's lifeless body on the floor.

"Tell me what I need to know, and you won't have to join him."

"Fuck you! I already died when you shot my son. I'm going to kill you, muthafucka! I swear to God," he said, sticking up his middle finger in Angel's direction.

Angel walked over to the man and aimed his gun at his face. The man closed his eyes and started praying in silence.

"It's funny how niggas always call on God when they get into trouble. Well, he can't help you now," Angel said, putting four bullets into the man's body and one into his head.

"We have to go, Angel. The cops are probably on their way and we don't need another shootout with them right now," his man said.

"Let's go!" Angel said as he motioned for everyone to leave.

They all rushed out the door and scattered into the vans, leaving another gruesome crime scene.

Angel called his boss and told him about the failed abduction and everything else. His boss wasn't mad, but he had given Angel specific instructions to carry out, and he hadn't. The boss told them to come back and let the goons continue to handle business. When Angel hung up the phone, he picked up the radio and gave everyone their orders: "Matar a todos los que tenían algo que ver con ella, y los echan a los tiburones (Kill all who had something to do with it, and throw them to the sharks)," he said angrily.

The other vans broke off and headed in another direction while Angel headed home. He had to go deal with his boss.

CHAPTER 15

Brandon and Hit-Man exited the SUV and shook hands with the two men who were still inside. They had just returned from making a meth deal. The money that Hit-Man had just made was going in with the rest of the money he received from all the other heists. He was going to break off with Brandon after paying him a hefty amount for getting him the buyers.

"Nice doing business with you guys. I'll let you know when I get some more work," Hit-Man told them.

"Okay, man. You have my number, so just hit me up."

Hit-Man said he would call them, but he knew his business was over with because he had sold all of the meth. The only way he would get more was if he really wanted to get into that part of the game. He gave Brandon his cut and hopped into his car to get back to Maysville. He had been gone for a few days and left his phone in the car.

As soon as he pulled it out from the center console, there were over thirty texts and eighty phone calls. He read the first text, which informed him that there was trouble. He needed to get to the spot. He first dialed Lit's phone.

"Where the fuck are you at, cannon?" Lit screamed as soon as the line connected. "You should know what the fuck is going on. It's because of you that we are at war with the fucking cartel! You need to hurry up and get back here. You have some shit to explain, bro and you have to be straight up with me. We already lost a lot of men. Vick and Gunz are locked up because of a witness. We have to take care of that and get those niggas out of there."

"I'll be there in about thirty minutes. See you soon," Hit-Man replied, ending the call.

Shit had just hit the fan, and now it was only going to get worse.

Hit-Man didn't know they were robbing the cartel. He thought about what the man said before he was killed, and now it made sense.

Fuck it, though. Those niggas can get it too. He thought as he hit the gas pedal to get back.

* * *

Lit was at one of the stash spots watching his workers package up the dope to distribute to the other blocks that were still operational. Since the war had started, they had been losing a lot of blocks, but they still had the main ones that his men guarded with their lives.

He and Hit-Man had a long conversation about his treacherous acts and how he was interfering with their money. Hit-Man explained to him that he was just trying to get at some sure fast money. Lit didn't care about what he was doing in the streets; he just wanted him to let him know so he could at least be on point in case something happened. He had Hit-Man's back regardless of the situation.

"I'll be back in a few, bro. I have to go drop off this money to Quana for the kids. We have to get back on track and handle our business. I'm going to set up a meeting with the cartel to try and squash this shit. You're fucking crazy, dawg. Out of all the niggas you could have robbed, you hit them." Lit smirked as he left the building.

He knew it wasn't as simple as he thought it was going to be, but he had to try something. If it didn't work, then fuck it. They would be going up against a whole fucking organization and most likely didn't have a chance of coming out alive.

Lit pulled up to Shaquana's crib and knocked on the door. She came to the door thinking it was her sister. When she opened it, her smile turned into anger.

"Why haven't you come to see your kids, Antonio?" She asked, calling him by his real name.

The only time she ever called him that was when she was mad.

"I told you there's a lot of shit going on right now, and I can't be around you and the kids without putting y'all in danger. Stay off my fucking back, okay!" He snapped, passing her an envelope full of cash.

"Take this shit! We don't need your money, Antonio! They need their father," she blurted out, throwing his money at him.

He left the money sitting on the floor and walked upstairs to see his kids. Shaquana quickly picked up the money and stuck it in a drawer. She knew the type of life that Lit was living when she first started dealing with him. She even thought about the day when she saved him from going to prison when he murdered someone right in front of her. She had driven the getaway car.

Shaquana looked around at the house that he bought for her and the kids and realized that he really took care of them. Even though they weren't together anymore, he made sure she and the kids didn't want for anything.

Lit came back downstairs a few minutes later and walked toward the door. Shaquana was sitting on the couch with her legs tucked underneath her.

"Are you gonna come back to see the kids later?" She asked, looking at him.

She really was trying to get him to stay with her.

"I told you what the deal was, Quana. I'll come get my kids when this beef is over. I can't put them in harm's way. There are some very bad people trying to get at us right now. I can't take that chance," he said as he walked out the door.

After what Shaquana did with his cousin, he knew he would never take her seriously again. He figured that since he was already in Birdsville, he would try to make amends with Doja. He stopped at a store and picked up a couple of things. When he got to Doja's house, her car was in the driveway. He got out and walked up to the door. He tried using his house key, but it didn't work. She had changed the locks when he left the last time. Lit knocked on the door, hoping that he didn't wake up her daughter. Two minutes later, Doja opened the door.

"What do you want, Antonio?" She said, with her hands on her hips.

Lit smirked because she also called him Antonio. It seemed like everyone did when they were angry with him.

He stared at her for a moment, taking in what she was wearing. Doja had on a pair of pajama shorts and a T-shirt that had "Suck Me" written across the chest.

"I got something for you," he stated, handing her a long box wrapped with a bow. "There's a rose for every month that you put up with my shit."

Doja wanted to smile, but she wasn't going to let him off the hook that easily. She dropped the roses on the ground and then walked away from the door.

Lit picked them up and stepped inside the house, closing the door behind him. Doja sat down at the kitchen table.

"Why are you here? You haven't been home in how long?" She asked, looking at him. "What? Your other bitch kicked you out, so now you want to come running back here?"

"I came to make up with you because I missed you too."

"You don't miss me, nigga. My daughter asks about you every day, and I tell her that you're out of town somewhere. You're making money now, so you don't need me anymore, huh? I rode your whole bid out with you and look how you do me?" She replied with tears coming out of her eyes. Lit didn't say anything. He knew he was wrong, and he wanted to make it up to her. He never meant to hurt her the way he did.

"Why don't you let me taste that pussy or are you gonna be mad at me forever?" He said, trying to put his hand between her legs.

"You ain't tasting anything, and how you come in here like everything is cool?" Doja replied, pushing his hand away.

But his touch had sent tingles through her body. She had to get away from him before she gave in.

"Come here, baby," he said, moving in so close that she could smell his breath.

He kissed her, and she kissed him back. When he saw that she wasn't resisting, he started sucking on her bottom lip. He lifted her up off the chair and walked into the living room. Lit sat on the couch as Doja straddled him. He removed her shirt to expose her titties. He had to admit. Her nipples were huge. He forgot what he was missing.

He sucked on them one at a time while pinching the other. Doja helped him remove his shirt and rubbed her hand over his six pack.

He smiled because he knew he had his girl back as he lifted her up off him.

He took off her slippers and gently began to suck on her toes. Doja sat there enjoying what was happening. She reached into her shorts and started to play with her pussy. It was so wet that when she pulled her hand out, it looked like she had stuck it into a cup of water.

"Baby! I need you to eat my pussy."

Lit removed her shorts and spread her legs. She closed her eyes anticipating his next move. He stuck a finger into her moistness and began fingering it while his tongue played with her clit. This drove her so crazy that she kept trying to get away from him. He had a firm grip on her legs, so she couldn't move. His tongue moved from her clit to her asshole and then back to her clit.

"Damn! You know how to work that tongue, nigga. I'm about to cum all over that shit," she said.

He looked up and started moving his tongue faster. He stuck another finger in and another inside until he had three fingers fucking her pussy. That shit sent her over the edge, and she came in his mouth. Lit drank all her juices without letting any spill out. He got up and looked at her lying there with her eyes closed. She was still shaking from the orgasm she just had. She opened her eyes after a minute and acted as if she had a sudden burst of energy.

"My turn," she said, pulling his dick out of his pants.

She got on her knees and slowly licked the tip. Then, she started blowing on it, driving him crazy this time. She took all ten inches into her mouth without even gagging once. Doja was showing him that she was also a beast at giving oral sex. Her head was moving up and down like a bobble head.

"I need to get up in that pussy before I blow my top," Lit moaned, pulling her body to the floor.

She bent over on the couch, spreading her wet pussy lips apart waiting for him to enter. At first, he took it easy on her, until she said, "Tear this pussy up, nigga!"

That's when he slammed into it and started blowing her back out. Doja bit down on her bottom lip while looking back at him beating it up. The look she gave him sent him over the edge. He felt himself ready to explode, and he turned her over onto her back. She opened her legs so wide that he thought he could see through her pussy hole.

He went right back to work, pumping in and out of her love tunnel. The only sound that could be heard was that of his balls hitting her ass cheeks. She grabbed her tits and started sucking on them while keeping an eye on his dick appearing and disappearing. She came again just as he was reaching his. He pulled out just in time to erupt all over her stomach.

"That was good, baby. You put that work in," Doja said, rubbing his head.

"I'm sorry that I hurt you, ma. A nigga had some shit to handle out in Maysville and it has me stressed out. You just helped me relieve some of that stress," he replied, sitting on the floor. "I'm not gonna lie to you. I have to go back out there because niggas trying me, but I had to make sure that you were good first. I can't have you in harm's way."

"When will you be back?" She asked, getting up and putting on her clothes in case her daughter got up and came downstairs.

"Just give me a couple of days, and I'll be back. You still have that burner I gave you, right?"

"Yeah, it's in my room."

"Put it in your purse and keep it with you at all times. If a nigga gets out of line, shoot first and ask questions last. Do you understand me?"

Doja nodded and watched as Lit fixed his clothes and tucked his gun into his pants. He gave Doja a kiss before leaving the house.

She walked out of her front door as he was just about to get into his car.

"Wait," she yelled out, walking up to him and passing him the spare key to her crib. "That's so you don't have to knock when you get home."

He smiled, gave her another kiss, hopped into his car and pulled off, heading to his next destination.

* * *

When he got to Truck's crib, he and Spade were sitting outside talking.

"What's up, nigga?" Spade said, giving him a pound, followed by Truck doing the same.

Spade was Truck's cousin from the other side of Birdsville. When Truck called him and told him that shit was about to jump off, he came over ASAP. They walked inside the house and went downstairs to the basement.

"I hope y'all niggas ready to go zero to a hundred real quick," Truck said.

Truck walked over to the light switch on the wall and flicked it off and on a couple of times. A couple seconds later, they watched as the wall slid to the side. The two hydraulic arms slowly made a low whistling sound to reveal a large vault-like room. The room was attached to the next door home's basement. Truck had bought the neighboring house and fixed it up. There wasn't an entrance to the basement there. You could only enter it through the secret wall.

"This is some movie type shit right here," Lit said, eyes wide open.

Inside the vault was damn near every gun you could think of. Truck had a bigger arsenal than Lit. There were rocket launchers, .45s, and different types of assault rifles.

"Where did you get this shit from?" Lit asked, picking up a pair of night-vision goggles.

"We hit a train a year ago and it had all types of military equipment on it. We grabbed as much as we could before the cops came," he explained.

"I remember hearing about something like that on the news. Fuck it, though. If these niggas want a ride, then let's do it!" Spade replied, strapping on a vest.

They geared up and Truck closed the vault back up before heading out. The three friends were about to go meet up with one of the top men in the cartel. Miguel had set up the meeting on the strength of Lit being one of his top buyers. He liked his business and hoped that it would continue to progress.

* * *

The meeting spot was at one of Miguel's restaurants. When Lit, Truck, and Spade arrived, they were escorted to the back, where Miguel was sitting on the couch smoking a Cuban cigar. He motioned for them to sit, but Lit declined, choosing to stand just in case shit went south.

"So, what would you like to talk about," asked Miguel. "I only agreed to this meeting because of Fisher. Are you the one who stole my product?"

"No," Lit replied, stepping forward with a duffel bag in his hand.

He dropped the bag at Miguel's feet. It landed with a hard thud on the floor. Lit stepped back, leaving it sitting there, before he spoke. "I don't know what happened with my man robbing your place, but I'm a man of honor," Lit began. "I would never betray the people who vouched for me, nor would I dirty my own or any of their names. A man's word is worth more than any dollar sign. That right there is every dollar you lost because of my man. I hope that brings peace between us, but if not, it's your move."

Miguel had to respect his gangsta. He cleared his throat, and about six coldhearted assassins came out of the back, wearing all-black fatigues. They had frowns on their faces and were holding assault rifles. They posted up around the room, covered all sides, and stood prepared to let their weapons bark on Miguel's command.

Lit and his two friends scanned the room. The odds were stacked against them, but that didn't mean shit. Lit wasn't fazed by any of the niggas in the room. The eyes don't lie, and he knew they were cold killers by theirs. He had seen those eyes before when his man came to talk to him. He was quite sure that's why everyone exited the room so quickly when he told them to get out. C.J. was a man who demanded respect, and now looking at Miguel and his goons, they demanded the same.

Lit wasn't the type to back down either. If he or anybody on his team was going to die, you'd best believe they were taking a couple of them with them. They all reached for their weapons, simultaneously gripping the handles.

The sounds of the click-clacks around the room echoed in harmony as Miguel's team peeped the move and clapped one in their chambers. Miguel's hand went up.

"Everybody chill the fuck out!" He shouted. "There is no need for bloodshed. Whoever pulls that trigger, even if it's by accident, will also have a bullet in their head before the other person's body hits the ground. Now stand down!"

The men did as their boss instructed. Lit and his two friends relaxed just a little bit but were ready to pop off at the first wrong movement. Miguel looked at Lit and then poured himself a drink.

"I know how niggas move. They fear what they can't understand, and they hate what they can't control," Miguel retorted.

"What is that supposed to mean?" Lit asked suspiciously, with his hand ready to pull out.

"Nothing. Nothing at all. Your friend disrespected me in the worst way. I need him to be held accountable for his actions."

"That's my man, so I'm riding with him no matter what. I'm trying to show you a peace offering, but if that's not good enough, then this meeting is over," Lit said confidently.

"Thank you for the gift, gentlemen. My men will show you out," Miguel said, downing the drink.

Lit didn't know what the dismissal meant, but he was going to prepare for whatever happened. They left the restaurant not as satisfied as he thought he would be. He made a mental note to give Fisher a call to find out if the war between them and the cartel was over or not. Deep down inside, he knew his team was no match for them, but pride would not let him just fold. Their reach was longer than the mobs, and he knew that they or their families could be touched anywhere they went.

Lit, Truck, and Spade got in the car and headed to West Maysville. There were some niggas out there who were also trying to get at Hit-Man. A birdie told one of their workers that the niggas with whom Hit-Man did business were going to rob and kill him.

Truck and Spade were ready to put in work tonight. They didn't want to go home without adding to the year's murder count.

"So, who is these other niggas that we have to go deal with?" Spade asked.

"Some niggas down the bottom in the campground. Hit-Man was fucking with them and robbing niggas. Now they trying to set him up, so we going to see what's good," Lit explained.

"Where that nigga at? He should be out here too, ready to handle his," Truck stated.

"I just texted him and told him to meet us at 40th and Indian Creek."

"Okay, cool," Truck said, sparking up some loud so they could get zooted on the way.

They rode in silence listening to Offset's *Open It Up*. They each had a Dutch of loud blowing as Lit cruised down Broad Street exit.

"If I should die don't cry my niggas. Just ride my niggas bust bullets in the sky my niggas. And when I'm gone, don't mourn my niggas. Just keep playing these songs my niggas. Say word to Sean my niggas."

* * *

When they went through Marine Street, nobody was out there. They parked on the next block and waited for a couple of hours. Hit-Man came and waited with them. He acted like everything was cool but Lit felt like he was too calm for someone who had a price on his head. His friend was really acting differently since the beef was squashed with the cartel. Lit just chalked it up to him being on his grind.

"Let's roll out. We'll catch these niggas another day," Lit said as he pulled off.

They were salty that they didn't get a chance to body anyone that night.

When Poochie had called Derrick and told him not to come home because niggas were out there trying to get him, he called P-Funk and let him know. When they tried to call Trey, he didn't answer his phone.

Later that night, they found out that the reason they hadn't heard from him was because he was dead. Someone had shot his car up when he and a couple of niggas were on their way to make a drug run. P-Funk thought he was trying to burn them and do shit on his own with their money.

Derrick took it hard because they were the closest of the three. The news said that it was some kind of drug hit by the way the car was shot up. Derrick and P-Funk thought it was from the robbery they did at the club, but how did they link it back to them? They had to watch their backs because shit was about to hit the fan, especially after Derrick got that call from the girl on his block saying that some niggas were waiting for them. They didn't know who it was or why they were looking for them.

"I think it's time to get out of Maysville, dawg. If niggas looking for us, it's only a matter of time before they find us because I'm not running," P-Funk stated, sitting in his crib on Franklin Avenue.

"I'm not running either. You were right about that nigga Hit-Man trying to get one over on us, too. We should have gotten his sneaky ass. I thought we were better than that," Derrick replied.

"Money changes everybody. That nigga is eating now and we still riding around in your sister's whip. After we body his ass and get that change he's sitting on, we out."

"Word. I'm with that," Derrick said as they remembered what Trey's mom said. They couldn't even give him a proper funeral and would have to cremate the body.

P-Funk didn't even respond. He was thinking about how bad he was going to do Hit-Man when he caught up with him. Finally, he would get to torture that nigga and then blow his brains out of his head.

"I'm about to go upstairs and handle some shit. Make yourself comfortable, nigga. There's a blanket over there in that bin. I'll see you in the morning," P-Funk chortled on his way upstairs.

Derrick chilled and played his PlayStation 5 all night while smoking loud. His gun rested right on his stomach for easy access just in case someone found them. He wasn't going to get caught slipping.

CHAPTER 16

Big Eazy lay in bed next to his girl, thinking about the chain of events that had taken place since he had been home. His girl's best friend had been killed, he had been shot and robbed, and now he found out that his own man had been the one responsible for it. On top of all that, his cousin had told him about coming up on some meth and that he was trying to get rid of it. The problem with that was his supplier had told him that someone had hit one of his clubs and gotten away with some work and money.

Big Eazy replayed that phone call his head. He felt as though Miguel needed to know what was going on. He wasn't stupid in any way. Hit-Man was Lit's friend, and he knew how Lit moved. Plus, he had that nigga Truck on his team with a bunch of young killers. It was only him and Drew, so he figured he would let Miguel's cartel eliminate Lit and his team. Then, he would take over all their territory. Miguel was no dummy though; he knew there had to be an ulterior motive behind Big Eazy's sudden actions, but he didn't care as long as he got all of his shit back.

"I have some distasteful news that I think you would find interesting," Big Eazy said.

"What is it?" asked Miguel.

"I know who was behind your club getting robbed," Big Eazy told him, waiting for a response.

"I'm listening," Miguel replied, tensing up at the thought of someone disrespecting him.

"It was some dude named Hit-Man. He was with a few dudes from West Maysville. One of the dudes is the one that tried to get with your niece. His name is Trey, and he lives right off of 75th and Williams."

"How do you know all this?" Miguel questioned him curiously.

If it was a setup, Miguel would kill Big Eazy and his family. In fact, just the thought of him snitching made Miguel want to cut out his tongue.

"My cousin told me that he was trying to move some meth for somebody. I remembered you saying that someone robbed one of your spots. I just put two and two together. How many people in Maysville know how to make meth? Look, I'm just letting you know what I found out," Big Eazy said.

"Thank you for the information. Someone will be dropping off something for you in about two hours," Miguel said, ending the call.

"Big Eazy, what's wrong?" Soshee asked, turning over and rubbing his chest.

"Nothing. I was just thinking about something. Those niggas that tried to murk me will be getting theirs sooner or later. They robbed some very dangerous people who take shit like that very personal."

"What does it have to do with you, though?" She asked, looking at him suspiciously.

"That's who supplies me with my work and helps me put food on the table or money in your pocket." He smirked, squeezing her ass when she stood up to put on her panties.

"I don't know, baby. However you look at it, that's still snitching, and we don't do that. What? He offer you something in exchange for it?" She asked.

"No, and that's not fucking snitching! Don't ever play me like that again," he replied aggressively.

"Don't get mad at me. Anyway, I'm going to my mother's house to take her out for her birthday. I'll be home later," Soshee stated, heading out of the door.

She loved Big Eazy, but she was from the streets too. She knew that he had snitched, regardless of what he called it. If muthafuckas in the hood got wind of it, they'd most likely say the same thing. She just shook her head as she cruised down the block bumping Lil Wayne.

* * *

Vick and Gunz had just been formally charged with two counts of murder and were now sitting in Metro Jail awaiting arraignment. There was only one way they would be able to beat their case, and that was getting rid of the witness. No witness means no trial, and no trial means no life sentences.

Detectives Eli and Washam were pleased that they finally got the people responsible for the double murder. They hoped Vick and Gunz rotted in prison with the possibility of no parole.

"Are you sure you don't want to relocate at the state's expense?" Washam asked. "You will have a new place to live and we'll give you a new identity."

"Why would I need all of that if they're in jail? I'm not scared of them anymore. Plus, my mom is sick, and I'm not leaving her here by herself. I'm good. Thank you for the offer, though," Kadeejah replied.

She got up from the desk and headed for the door, slinging her handbag over her shoulder. Detective Washam followed her outside to talk to her some more. A car was parked in front of the station, waiting for her.

"If you need me for anything, just give me a call. I don't care if it's day or night," Washam told her, passing Kadeejah her card. "See you at trial."

Kadeejah took the card without saying anything. She just gave Washam a head nod and got into the waiting car.

As they drove off, she couldn't help but think about the long process that a drawn-out trial would take. She hoped they took a deal so she wouldn't have to testify.

"What happened?" Her cousin asked, looking over at her as they waited for the light to change.

"Nothing. Somebody broke into my neighbor's house, and I had to give them a statement since I called them," she lied.

"Oh, okay. Are we still going out tonight? They are having a party for my homegirl. She's about to get married next month."

"Oh, of course. I'm game. What time are you coming to pick me up?"

"Girl, just meet me at my crib around nine thirty. We'll pick up my friend and leave from there," the girl replied, pulling up in front of Kadeejah's mom's house. "

See you then," Kadeejah said as she exited the car.

When the girl pulled off, she made a very important call. When the person on the other end answered, she spoke briefly.

“She’s going with me tonight. We will be there to pick you up around nine forty-five. Grab some loud from your boy so we can get fucked up,”

“I got you, and I’ll be sitting outside waiting for you when y’all get here,” the caller said, and hung up.

* * *

Hit-Man was in too deep with the shit he was doing. He knew if he didn’t stop, money wouldn’t be made because they would be too busy beefing with niggas. He had just gotten off the phone with Lit and was leaving out the door so he could go check on the stash spot in Prichard. When he pulled off, so did another car. The driver stayed far enough behind so he could see where Hit-Man was going but also not be noticed.

As soon as they got on the expressway, the car sped up and tried to catch up with Hit-Man. As soon as the driver was right behind Hit-Man’s car, he hit the sirens, signaling for him to pull over.

“What the fuck these pigs want with me? I ain’t doing shit,” Hit-Man said as he slowed down and pulled over.

The officer got out of the car and walked over to the driver’s window. He motioned for Hit-Man to roll down his window. The whole time he had his hand on the handle of his gun. Hit-Man did as he was asked, to see what the officer wanted.

“What did I do, Officer? Why did you pull me over? I’m late for an appointment.”

“If you don’t shut the fuck up, you’ll be even later. Now, can I see your license, registration, and insurance card, please?”

Hit-Man reached into the glove compartment, being careful not to make any erratic movements to cause the trigger-happy pig to shoot him. He gave the officer all the paperwork and watched as he read it over.

“Can you turn off the engine and step out of the car, sir?” The officer asked.

“This is some bullshit right here. I haven’t done anything wrong,” Hit-Man said, stepping out of his car.

"Put your hands on the hood of the car, please."

Hit-Man did as he was directed. The officer patted him down to make sure he didn't have any weapons on him. He then asked Hit-Man to step over to his unmarked car. He placed Hit-Man in the backseat while he went to search his car. After checking out the car, the officer returned and let Hit-Man out of his unmarked car.

"Sorry for the trouble, sir. You have a good day," the officer said as he walked back to his car and pulled off.

Hit-Man got back into his car and picked up the white envelope that was now sitting on the passenger seat. He opened it and smiled as he read its contents. He had what he was waiting for to take care of business. Having cops on the payroll was really paying off for them.

He had told Lit that he wouldn't do anything crazy again that would put them in a situation like they had been in, without putting him up on game. But this was different. This had to be taken care of, and soon. He made the call to his worker, sharing the information that he just received, and told him to handle it.

After checking on his spots, Hit-Man decided to stop over at one of his shorties' cribs. He pulled up in front of Shekema's house and saw that her car was there. He got out and walked up to the door. He didn't have to knock, because he had a key that she had given him when they first met.

Hit-Man entered the house and walked into the kitchen. He smiled when he saw that she was wearing nothing but a thong and bra. Her shapely legs, juicy behind, and slim waist instantly sent sparks to his loins. The stilettos that graced her french-manicured toes caused him to smile even harder. He removed his gun from his waist and sat it on the kitchen table. He walked up behind her and wrapped his arms around her, burying his head in the creases of her shoulder as he inhaled deeply, loving the scent coming from her body.

"I could have slumped you just now. You didn't even know I was here," he whispered as he kissed her neck.

Shekema's head fell to the side as she enjoyed the feel of his lips against her skin.

"Hmmmm. That feels good," she moaned.

She turned toward him and kissed his lips deeply and sensuously.

"A nigga will never catch me slipping. Take a look under the towel on the counter."

Shekema slipped out of his embrace and walked over to grab something from the refrigerator. Hit-Man lifted up the towel and saw the Glock lying underneath it.

He chuckled and thought to himself, *This is one bad bitch.*

Shekema took everything seriously since being shot in the head while sitting on her porch. She carried her strap everywhere she went. He found her incredibly sexy. The fact that she was a rider impressed him. She had the street instincts of a nigga, and he liked that.

"Have a seat if you want something to eat," she said.

"What you cook?" Hit-Man asked, taking a seat.

"Steak and potatoes."

"And for dessert?"

"Me," she answered.

Shekema straddled him in the chair. The only thing stopping her wet pussy from soaking the crotch of his pants was the tiny fabric from her thong.

"Or you can have your dessert now," she seductively said.

Hit-Man sat her on the table after pushing everything out of the way. He removed his manhood, and in one movement, he slid her thong to the side. Her wetness warmed him as he slipped inside her. With one arm wrapped around her waist and the other bracing the table, he controlled the pace. He was slow stroking her as their bodies moved rhythmically.

"Yes, baby," she moaned as he kissed her neck.

His dick penetrated the depth of her that she didn't know existed. Hit-Man's sex game was official. Each stroke made her hornier and hornier, and with every dip of his hips, she matched his intensity. She ground upward and threw her pussy at him as their bodies became one.

Hit-Man knew she had the best pussy around. That's why he always kept her on speed dial. If he wasn't out there doing dirt all the time, he would have wifed her. Only a few people had the privilege of sampling it, because even though she was in the streets, she wasn't a whore.

She closed her eyes and enjoyed the ride as she felt her orgasm build. She came so hard that she lost her breath for a moment. The pulsating tool inside her, along with the look of fulfillment on Hit-Man's face, told her that he had gotten his too.

"Wow, I don't think I'm going to be able to eat now after that," Hit-Man stated, fixing his clothes.

"Well come upstairs and let me give you the whole performance," Shekema said, heading toward the steps.

She made her ass cheeks twerk to get Hit-Man's attention. Hit-Man grabbed the bottle of Patron off the table and followed her up the steps. He couldn't wait to get some more of that pussy. She had him sprung.

* * *

Kadeejah and her cousin pulled up on Fishers Alley to pick up her friend so they could head to the club. He went inside Exxon to get something to drink. When he came out, he got in the backseat.

Here. Blaze up," he said, passing them both a game filled with loud. They sparked them up and took a couple of pulls.

"Damn, this shit is fire," Kadeejah stated, taking another pull.

"I told you my nigga only got that good shit," Kadeejah's cousin replied. "You want some of this Henny?"

"I'm good," the bull said, leaning back in the seat.

He had the Dutch in one hand while he was texting with the other.

After they smoked the loud, Kadeejah was feeling it. She closed her eyes and bobbed her head to the music. Her cousin finished drinking the Henny, and they were ready to get their groove on.

The dude they were with was sitting right behind Kadeejah, who was sitting in the passenger seat. He smoothly removed his gun that was tucked in his waist and placed it on his lap. He would have only a split second to complete the task, so he had to make it count.

He held up the gun against the seat and let off two quick shots.

Boc! Boc!

Kadeejah's body slumped over in the seat. Her cousin screamed and tried to jump out of the car. He aimed the gun at her and squeezed off a round into her back.

Boc!

Her body fell to the ground, and she started crawling and trying to get away. He leaped out of the car and ran over to where she was.

"Please don't kill me. I have a daughter. I promise I won't say anything," she pleaded.

"I know you won't," he said, letting off four more shots into her body. "Nothing personal; it's just business."

Next, he went over to make sure Kadeejah was dead. He pumped two more rounds into her head. He was about to run, when two undercover cops jumped out of a car, with their guns in hand.

"Freeze! Police!" one of them shouted.

"Drop the gun now and put your hands in the air!" The female officer ordered.

She noticed that he wasn't ready to comply, so she placed her finger on the trigger. It was too late. He already had the drop on her.

Boc! Boc! Boc! Boc! Boc! Boc!

Shots rang out, and Detective Washam hit the ground. She wasn't wearing a vest, so three of the bullets ripped right through her stomach and arm. She let out a loud yelp and put her hand over the hole where blood was gushing out.

Detective Eli saw his partner go down, and the suspect started to run away. Eli let off four shots in the suspect's direction, dropping him in the middle of the street. He ran toward the man lying on the ground.

The suspect tried to turn over and point the gun at the approaching detective.

"Drop it!" Eli yelled.

But he didn't, so Detective Eli fired a kill shot to his head and kept on shooting until his clip was empty.

More cops were approaching the scene in a hurry. You could hear the sounds getting closer and closer. Eli ran back over to where his partner was lying on the ground. He started applying pressure to the wound. Cops started jumping out of cars and rushing over to where they were.

"We have to get her to a hospital now! Help me get her into the car!" He shouted.

Two officers immediately helped him pick her up and get her into one of the cars. Detective Eli hopped into the driver's seat and sped off to get his partner to UAB Hospital. Even though it wasn't a trauma unit anymore, they tried to do everything to save her life because she was a police officer. Detective Washam died forty-five minutes later from all the blood she lost and the bullet that kept circulating through her body.

CHAPTER 17

"A deadly shooting has left four people dead, including a police officer. Witnesses say they heard shots around ten-thirty last night, and when they peeped out of the window, they saw a man running from the scene and falling face-down. Then, a plain-clothed officer ran up on him and shot him at least ten times. We'll have more on this shooting as details come in. I'm Sharon Williamson with Fox 10 news. Back to you.

"What happened?" Vick said, rushing over toward the television on the block he was on.

"Some nigga was murked by the police last night. He shot an undercover cop in the process, though. That muthafucka went out like a G," the young bull said as they continued to watch the breaking news.

"I hope Gunz is over there watching this shit. We might be going home sooner than we thought," he stated.

"Why you say that?"

"Nothing. Those cops were on our case. I think they were dirty and tried to set us up," Vick replied.

He didn't want to tell him the real reason he would be getting out. You never know who the rats are in jail, until you feed them some cheese. That's when they come out from the cracks of the walls and show their true sides.

"Damn. They probably were dirty. Look at all the shit going on out in Ferguson. They just shot and burned an activist, and everyone thinks it was a hate crime. But I think the cops had something to do with it because they didn't like what he was out there fighting for," the dude said.

"You may have a point, but I'm not into that debating shit right now. I have to go holla at my man on the other block. I'll get at your later," Vick said, walking back to his cell to put on his blues.

He grabbed his blue shirt and was about to walk out the door, when two guys walked in. They both were carrying something in their hands. They pulled the door closed, making sure they didn't lock themselves in. Vick noticed that what they were carrying were homemade shanks.

"You robbed the wrong muthafucka, dawg," one of them said as they were mean-mugging Vick.

Vick looked at both men and knew he was not match for both of them. He would be able to take the skinny one, but the other dude was huge. He couldn't even get to his banger that was tucked under the bed.

"I don't know what you talking about, but whatever you want to do, let's get it," he replied, showing no signs of backing down.

The two dudes started toward Vick, and he popped off, attacking them first. He caught the little one with a haymaker, which only stunned him for a second. The big dude grabbed Vick by the throat and started poking him in the stomach with the shank he had in his hand. The other dude followed up after catching his composure. They continuously poked Vick over and over again. Blood was everywhere, but they didn't stop until someone knocked on the door, letting them know that a corrections officer was walking around.

The two men immediately rushed out of the cell and ran into their own, changing their clothes that had blood all over them. They took the bloody clothing and tried to flush it down the toilet. After they changed, they walked out on the tier and sat down like nothing had happened.

Corrections Officer Smith was making her rounds that she usually did when she came on the block. When she reached the second tier and walked past Vick's cell, she stopped with a look of horror on her face.

"Oh my God!" she screamed. "Code red! Code red!" she radioed as she looked into the room.

She rushed inside and tried to see if Vick was still alive. Fellow officers started to flood the block.

"Everybody lock in! Now!" The lieutenant yelled out as other officers started banging doors.

The medical department rushed onto the block with a stretcher to get the wounded man. It was already too late, though, because Vick died in the arms of Corrections Officer Smith. They still tried shocking him and performing CPR while they wheeled him out on the gurney, to make it look good in the eyes of the other inmates. They already knew the deal when niggas got stabbed up.

Gunz was on the next block when they saw all the corrections officers running over to the block. He and a couple of other niggas from around his way were trying to see what had happened, when the COs on the block made them lock in. He wanted to make sure his man was good, but they threatened to lock him up if he didn't lock in.

"I'm already locked up! What are you gonna do? Put me in the hole?" He said sarcastically.

The corrections officer that worked the block knew Gunz was on trial for two murder cases and didn't really give a fuck where he was housed, so he tried to calm down the situation. "I will let you know if your friend is okay. Just go ahead and lock in," he said, hoping Gunz would follow his order peacefully.

Gunz went to his cell and just missed them rushing past with his friend's body.

Later on that day, they moved Gunz from the prison because they thought he was next. He found out his friend was dead, and snapped, trying to fight the guards as they tried to cuff him. He ended up in the hole over at Draper.

* * *

It had been three days since the prison had gone on lockdown. An investigation on who murdered Vick was still underway, with no leads. The warden finally cleared the lockdown, and the inmates were able to come out and take showers or use the phone again.

"Yo. That situation is done, but we couldn't get at the other dude 'cause they moved him," C.D. said.

"Where they move him to?"

"Over to Fountain."

"Okay. That money will be in your account in about an hour. Let King know we got him, too," the person on the phone stated. "Oh, and don't say shit on this jack again. You niggas are stupid in there. They record everything just so they can use it against you. I'm glad you didn't say my name or we would be having problems," the guy said before he hung up.

C.D. went over to where King was gambling and whispered in his ear. King nodded and continued playing cards. After the game was over, he headed over to where C.D. was standing.

"Yo! We need to try and hurry up and get out of here before they find out it was us," C.D. said.

"Yeah, I wish we could have gotten to that other nigga before they found him."

"We should have just hung that muthafucka. It would have been less gruesome, and the pigs wouldn't have found him so quickly."

"Maybe, but let's get your people on the horn since they're closer to paying that bail. My people are all the way out in Allentown," King said.

C.D.' s real name was Clifton Deeds, and he was from North Mobile. He had a crib on 12th Street, until he got locked up on a gun charge. He couldn't pay his bail because his girl ran off with another nigga. They took all of it with them. That's why when this opportunity presented itself, he took it ASAP.

King went by the name Miami or Kenneth Bedgood, and he was born and raised in New York, but he recently moved to Mobile. He was on his way to pull a job with a couple of friends in Mobile, when they got pulled over. The cops ran Jail.

His boys received million-dollar bails because they had bodies on them. King's bail was $ 200,000, so when C.D. told him that someone needed them to put some work in, he agreed. They were cellmates and that's how their bond was formed.

"You make the call, and I'm going to use the bathroom before they try to lock us back up," King stated as he headed for his cell.

C.D. made the call to his people to let them know to post his and King's bails. The dude that hired them was going to put them on. They hoped they would be out by tomorrow so this shit wouldn't hold them.

* * *

When Gunz called Hit-Man and gave him the news about Vick, he just shook his head like it really didn't mean shit. It was Lit who was pissed that one of his men got touched. He wanted to get at whoever did it, to let them know that when someone touched one of theirs, he'd touch ten of theirs.

Lit sent word inside the jail for information on who had something to do with the hit on Vick. He was just waiting for them to get back to him. He even put a price on their heads.

Hit-Man was sitting outside of a familiar crib with one of his men. He had met him when he signed the papers that released him from probation.

"As soon as you walk in the door, look to the right, and you will see it. Just grab the whole thing and get out of there. Here!" he said, passing him $400. "That's half now, and I'll give you the rest when you come out with the safe."

The man nodded and got out of the car. He walked into the building and headed up the steps. When he found the apartment he was looking for, he pulled out a piece of metal wire and stuck it into the lock.

Soshee was just getting out of the shower when she heard someone at the door. As she walked toward it, she noticed that whoever it was was trying to pick the lock. She tiptoed over to the door and looked through the peephole. A man with a hoodie over his head was on the other side. Soshee ran to her bedroom and into the walk-in closet. She looked around until she found the box she was looking for. She quickly pulled out the .44 Bulldog that Big Eazy had kept in it and checked to see if it was loaded. The gun that he had bought her was in her purse, which she had left in the car.

Thinking that the intruder was about to open the door, she aimed the gun and waited with her finger on the trigger. When the first lock clicked, it startled her, and she squeezed the trigger.

Boom!

The gun knocked her on her ass as the bullet went straight through the door.

“Aghhh!” The man screamed out in pain as the bullet hit him in his shoulder.

He ran down the steps trying to get away.

Hit-Man heard the shot and immediately pulled out his burner from under the driver’s seat. He looked at the front door and waited to see what had happened. Seconds later, the dude came running out holding his arm. He jumped into the car and Hit-Man pulled off.

“What happened up there?” He said.

“Somebody heard me and shot through the door. My fucking arm hurts, man. I need to get to a hospital.”

Hit-Man was pissed that his plan hadn’t worked. There was no way he was taking him to a hospital, though. He drove until he came upon a cemetery right off of Baltimore Avenue.

“Yo! Grab the first aid kit out of the trunk,” he told the guy as he pulled over.

The guy got out of the car and walked in back toward the trunk. Hit-Man opened the door and held his gun down next to his thigh. He looked around to make sure no one was around, and then aimed the gun at the guy’s head.

“Wait! What you doing, man?”

“No witnesses. Sorry, bro,” he said as he shot him in the head.

He died before he hit the ground. Hit-Man jumped back into the car and peeled off. But he was pissed off because he didn’t get what he wanted.

CHAPTER 18

Lit was sitting in Big Daddy's waiting for Hit-Man to arrive. Lately, it seemed like they were having a power struggle on who was in charge. He wanted to lay all the cards on the table once and for all. They were equal in his eyes, but he was a better businessman than Hit-Man. Hit-Man didn't know how to move large quantities of work. He was the type to probably blow it more than get rich. That's why Lit took care of all the deals.

Lit kept looking at his watch and wondering why Hit-Man hadn't yet arrived. He already had been there for over an hour. Time was everything, and right now, time was something that Lit didn't have a lot of.

"Man, fuck this shit. I'm outta here," Lit said, putting a fifty-dollar bill on the table and getting up to leave.

As he walked out, Hit-Man pulled up at the corner and honked his horn.

Beep! Beep!

"Yo, bro! Sorry I'm late. I got caught up in traffic."

"Man! You got me bloody as shit right now, dawg. You really on some sucka shit right now. What, you couldn't hit my phone and let me know this?" he said, standing next to Hit-Man's car.

"Get in. I have to tell you something, bro, seriously," Hit-Man replied.

Lit hopped in the passenger seat as Hit-Man pulled into the parking lot.

"So! What the fuck do you have to tell me, man? I'm trying to get money, and all this dumb shit you're into right now is stopping that shit," Lit said.

Hit-Man began telling him about the Big Eazy situation and what had happened with his man trying to grab the safe from his girl's crib. Hit-Man listened as Lit told him how stupid that shit was and that he should have waited to do that. Now he had no choice but to kill Big Eazy and his people. Lit thought long and hard and formulated a plan in his head.

"You go grab the money from the spots, and I'll take care of this Big Eazy situation. We have no more room for error, or our big homie is going to dead our supply. I'm not going out like that," Lit told him, getting out the of the car.

"If you need me, just call."

"I'm good. I can handle this shit by myself," Lit replied as he walked off. "Call Chloe. She's going to ride with you to take care of business."

Hit-Man was really getting frustrated with the fact that Lit always wanted Chloe to handle shit. He thought long and hard about just putting a bullet in her head to alleviate the middleman altogether, but that would only stir up some more shit. Besides, that was only a thought. He would never do something like that.

"Well, since he wants to handle shit, I'll just let her take care of that, and I'll go get me something to drink," he said to himself.

He called Chloe's phone and told her to go pick up the money from the spots and to call him after she was done. After talking to her, he made another call before getting out of his car and going into the bar. He was going to wait for Chloe to bring the money to him, and then he would hand it over to Lit.

* * *

Hit-Man, Chloe, and Lit were standing outside of the Springhill Suites Apartment complex waiting for two people that they hired to handle some business. Poncho opened the door and invited them inside. When they walked in, Xavier was sitting at the table cleaning guns.

"I see you still on some mob shit." Chloe smiled.

"Couldn't have it any other way. You know that prison shit is not gonna change a nigga like me. The streets is my life, and I'd rather be carried out by six than to be judged by twelve," Xavier stated, standing up and giving her a hug. "You still look good."

"I know," she replied while spinning around. "Anyway, these are my peoples I was telling you about. Lit and Hit-Man, this is

Bricks and Poncho. These dudes will put in any kind of work you need."

"What's up, cannon?" Hit-Man said, shaking their hands. Lit followed up with greetings as well.

"There's a couple niggas out there that I'm not feeling right now, and I would like you to eliminate them. If we do it ourselves, the law will be all over this. I'm not sure what they know, but for some reason, my name has been coming up within the federal building. Now I have to lay low from putting my murder game down," Lit said.

"Do you think it has anything to do with the fact that your man has been out there sticking muthafuckas up?" Poncho asked, looking at Hit-Man.

Both Hit-Man and Lit were caught off guard with the comment. Bricks knew where that statement was going to lead, and he had his hand on his strap.

"Don't look so surprised. We hear everything. Those cartel niggas was gonna cut your hands off and feed them to their dogs, but your man stood up for you. They respect him, but not you," Poncho continued.

"We didn't come here for that! So can everyone put their testosterone to the side right now. We are all on the same team, and we both don't like this nigga Big Eazy. So let's get at him," Chloe said.

"I'm with that. He killed my brother, and for that, I'll kill him and his family for free," Bricks said.

"Leave his family be. Just get that nigga, and if you working for me, then you will never be working for free. This is for you," Lit said, tossing both of them a thick envelope. "Plus, that building next door belongs to y'all. Just cop from me, and you can do as you please."

Xavier and Poncho looked at each other and nodded in agreement. The deal was now set, and they would be up for the task. That gave Lit and his crew the opportunity to really focus on their investments and deals. Lit was looking into some buildings to buy and fix up. He wanted to put Birmingham back on the map and bring some money to his city. Lit, Hit-Man, and Chloe left the apartment feeling confident that Poncho and Xavier would handle their business.

"Chloe, since they are your people, they're your responsibility. I know you wouldn't just recommend them if they weren't about their business but keep an eye on them. Hit-Man, did you contact your connect in the federal building yet to see what's up?" Lit asked as they headed for their cars.

"Let's get the fuck out of this place before we get blamed for it!" King stated as they headed out. Big Eazy ran into Kayla's bedroom and went into the closet. He opened the safe that they had moved from Soshee's crib, and took out everything, putting it into one of her big bags that was hanging up. He went into her son's room and removed the lamp, slamming it on the floor and trying to rush. He took the packs of ecstasy out and also put them in the bag. After grabbing everything he had there, he ran out and got into the car. They pulled off and headed to Big Eazy's spot. Using Kayla's phone, Big Eazy made an anonymous call to the cops about the bodies before he left and left it off the hook so they could trace the call. That was the least he could do. They rode in silence as they headed for Big Eazy's crib. King drove, and Woody sat in the backseat. King had been plotting the whole time they were driving. When they pulled up into Big Eazy's garage, King snapped. He pulled out his gun. Big Eazy didn't even see it coming because he was lost in his own thoughts.

Boom!

The shot entered the side of Big Eazy's head, and his body went limp instantly. King knew he was dead from the first shot, but he hit him again for good measure.

"Come on! Let's get the shit and get the fuck back so we can relax, man. All this shit has got me tired as hell," Woody said, digging into Big Eazy's pockets for his keys.

"You go ahead. I have to make it look good, and then I'll get the car," King replied.

Woody ran up in the crib to grab the rest of the work and money while King staged the scene to look like a suicide, not evening realizing that he had shot him twice. As he walked to get the car that they had parked down the street, he made a phone call.

"It's done!" King said, when the caller answered.

"Good. Your prioritizing this will be rewarded. Check your mailbox in the morning," the caller stated before ending the call. King got in the car and pulled up in front of the door to help Woody with the work and money hidden all through the house. They took everything and got out of there.

* * *

Miguel ended the call and sat back in his chair with a grin on his face. He looked over to one of his lieutenants and lit his Cuban cigar.

"One puta down, and two more to go! By this time next month, everyone will bow down to the cartel," he said, hitting the table with his fist. His men nodded in agreement as they lifted their glasses and toasted to victory.

CHAPTER 19

"Damn, baby. Don't stop!" Doja begged breathlessly, opening her legs wider to give Lit more access to her love tunnel.

She hadn't been sure it was possible, but she was able to place her legs all the way back, touching her ears as he practically pushed his entire face inside her pussy lips. The way he was sucking on her clit almost made her cum instantly. His tongue game was on point, and Doja was speechless at the moment. There was nothing in the world that could keep her quiet the way Lit could with his tongue licking, sucking, and flicking through the folds of her pussy.

"Mmmmm," Lit hummed into her dripping wet box, tasting the strawberry flower coming from it.

His head game caused so much pleasure that Doja almost felt dizzy. She closed her eyes tight as he started lightly kissing her up and down her swollen clit. Every time he pushed his face into it, it made a sucking noise when he pulled away. Doja couldn't take it anymore. She needed some good dick, and she wanted it now.

"Baby, please," she mumbled, with her eyes still closed, holding his head. "I want to feel you inside me now!" She felt Lit pull back before sticking two fingers inside of her pussy. Then, she felt his warm mouth over her right nipple, sucking on it while he squeezed the other with his free hand. She almost screamed out loud, but she didn't want to wake her daughter. Her body started jerking, and although she didn't want to, she was about to cum.

"Not yet," he ordered. "You better not do it until I say so!"

He pulled his fingers out and removed his mouth from her breast. Doja opened her eyes and caught a glimpse of him right before his dick entered her pussy, pushing her walls open even wider than she was ready to go at that moment.

The first thing that came to her mind was to meet his every thrust, but she was no match for him. He was tearing that shit up, and she loved the way he put it down. He was definitely winning.

"Oh shit, baby! I can't take it anymore. Shit! Tear this up," she moaned loudly.

Lit's phone started blowing up. He and Doja both groaned at the sound. She stopped moving her body so he could get up.

"Fuck. I thought I had it on vibrate," he said. "I'm not going to answer it yet. Whoever it is can wait."

Lit began pounding away again at her pussy like he was in a rush to bust his nut. Doja wrapped her legs around his waist and gave it back. They were in sync with their movements. She smiled in pleasure at the fact that he was putting her needs over his business affairs. The phone started ringing again.

"Aggghhh." Doja laughed. "Just go ahead and answer it, 'cause it's killing my vibe."

Lit grabbed his phone and shook his head as soon as he saw the screen. He didn't need to talk to them right now. He knew they were about their business, so he could speak with them later about the issue. When it rang once more, he figured something was up, so he answered.

"What's up?" He said, walking out of the bedroom and out of earshot of Doja so she couldn't hear his conversation.

"We had a problem with your car," Xavier said, speaking in code just in case their phones were tapped.

"Where you at now?"

"Down the street from your man Truck's crib."

"Okay. Go there and wait for me. I'm on my way now. I'll call Truck and tell him to let you in," Lit replied, ending the call.

He wanted to know what had happened.

He went back into the room and got dressed. Doja could tell something was wrong from the look on his face. She didn't press the issue, though, because no matter what, she supported her man.

After getting dressed, Lit gave Doja a kiss and rushed out the door. When he got into his car, he checked his clip to make sure it was fully loaded. He just wanted to be prepared for whatever happened.

A few minutes later, he was parking outside of Truck's house. As soon as he walked in, Truck, Poncho, and Xavier were sitting there with blank expressions on their faces. There was a lot of tension in the room, so Truck spoke first to try to ease it before Lit got the news.

"We have Birmingham on smash now, bro. Everyone is buying from us, and if they're not, I'm sure I don't have to finish that statement," he said, giving Lit a smile.

"That's great and all, but I know you didn't call me all the way over here to tell me that, so what is it?" Lit asked, looking at Xavier and Poncho.

"We had a problem with getting the whereabouts of that nigga Big Eazy, and we ended up killing his bitch," Xavier began.

"Shit happens. She became a casualty of war. Did you at least get that nigga?"

"Almost! But he got away before we could kill him. His men was with him, and we only bodied one of them. We are going back through his neighborhood tomorrow though," Poncho mentioned.

"No! Go past there tonight, and if you need more men, take some. I want him dead by tomorrow morning," Lit said.

"There's more," Xavier started, not ready to tell him, but Lit gave him a look to continue. "His bitch sister and son were also there, and you know the rules of the streets: no witnesses. They had to go because they seen our faces."

They all looked at Lit, waiting for a reaction to the news that Xavier had just dropped on him. Lit didn't want any kids dying, but he also knew that if they had left them alive, there was a chance of them going away for the rest of their lives. No one could risk that.

"Fuck 'em! They shouldn't have been there. Call me when that nigga joins them. I'll have something nice ready for both of you," Lit said, throwing in another incentive besides what he already had already given them.

"Will do," Xavier replied. "We have shit to do, so we're out of here. That nigga will be joining his bitch soon."

They left out the door to handle business. Poncho and Xavier didn't want to tell Lit the torturous things they had done to the little boy. They didn't want him to think about his own kids being tortured like that. If he did find out, it wouldn't be from them, and they wanted to get Big Eazy in the worst way. Little did they know that

Big Eazy was already dead by the hands of his own men, or who he thought were his men. They were hired by an organization higher than any of them could ever imagine.

The next day when Xavier was watching television, a breaking news story came across the screen informing that Big Eazy was found shot to death inside of a car in front of his house. Xavier called Poncho and informed him of the news. They were mad that they hadn't gotten the chance to put the bullet in him, but they were happy it was done. Xavier decided to make it seem like they were the ones that put the work in. He figured Lit wouldn't care as long as it was done.

* * *

T-Baby was on a Greyhound on his way back to his old stomping grounds. He was just released from prison after getting his sentence overturned. It came so unexpectedly that he didn't even get a chance to call anyone. They made him rush to pack up and get his discharge papers signed. The real reason was they didn't want a lawsuit for holding him too long. He was sitting in the back of the bus by himself. When he looked up, he noticed a beautiful woman sitting in front of him playing a game on her phone.

"Excuse me. Could I use your phone real quick to call somebody to meet me at the bus stop?" He asked, getting her attention.

"Sure," she replied, handing it to him.

T-Baby called his brother and told him he was on his way to home and to meet him at the bus station. At first, his brother thought he was lying, but when he heard people talking in the background, he believed what his brother had said. When he hung up, he passed the phone back to the woman. He also noticed that she was listening to his conversation.

"Thank you. I'm just coming home from prison. I was locked up for a crime I didn't commit. They finally figured it out and released me," he explained.

"Damn. That's crazy. Were you down for a while?" She asked.

"Just a little while, but I'm good. Anyway, what is your name, and where you from?"

"Meesha, and I'm from Atlanta. I'm going to Montgomery to see a couple of friends. I just came home too. I was locked up for three years."

"Oh shit. So you just come home and already got a phone, huh?"

"Yeah," she said sarcastically but playfully. "I came home yesterday, but my friend wanted me to come down there. She wired me the money for a phone and bus ticket. I'm only staying for a week."

T-Baby moved up to where she was sitting and sat next to her. He wanted to get to know her. Meesha was about five four, and she had brown eyes, a little thickness, and nice titties. She was a white girl, and T-Baby wanted to see what she was about.

"So, do you have a boyfriend?" he asked.

"No, I'm single. So, what about you? Do you have a girl?"

"I did, but she thought I was never coming home and stepped off with the next nigga. I'm Muslim, so I need to find me a wife, but she has to be on her deen," he replied, looking at her with lust in his eyes.

They sat and talked the whole ride, until the bus made a pit stop so everyone could stretch their legs and get something to eat. Once they got their food, they got back on the bus. T-Baby kept looking at her ass in the sweatpants she was wearing. His dick got hard just from thinking about what he wanted to do to her.

Since they both were fresh out, he tried to push up on her. To his surprise, she told him that she needed some dick bad. Since nobody was sitting back there near them, T-Baby told her to turn sideways. He pulled her sweatpants down and fucked her right there with no condom. Neither of them took one second to think about the other having anything. When they finished, both of them fixed their clothes as if they hadn't done anything.

The two of them conversed for the remainder of the ride, talking about different topics. By the time they reached Cone Street, it seemed as if they had known each other for a long time. Meesha gave him her phone number and told him to hit her up tomorrow so they could have a round two. He stepped out of the bus terminal, and P-Funk and Derrick were standing next to a car waiting for him.

"Lil nigga, what's up?" P-Funk said, walking toward his brother. They hadn't seen each other in a while, and he was glad that he didn't have to do the time.

"I'm good, bro. Glad to be home."

They gave each other dap followed by a hug. P-Funk stepped back to take in his little brother.

"Somebody been working out in that joint?" P-Funk said, noticing how big T-Baby had gotten.

"I had to get my weight up in there. Just in case one of these niggas tried to get stupid out here," he replied.

P-Funk thought about telling him about the beef they had just encountered. But he decided to wait until later. Right now, they were going to get fucked up.

"You don't have to worry about that. Niggas know what it is in these streets," Derrick said.

"Here, take this," P-Funk told T-Baby, passing him a burner. "Just so you're ready and don't have to get ready."

"Get in, y'all. Let's get the fuck out of here and go chill with some bitches," Derrick said.

They all hopped in the car and pulled out into traffic. P-Funk sparked up the loud while T-Baby popped open the bottle of E&J. They headed to the After Hour on Ann, a club that P-Funk had helped open down the bottom with his man JoJo.

The place was packed when they got there. T-Baby got fucked up with his brother all night. He was going to get in touch with his older brother the next day to get back on. He just hoped that he wouldn't be on some bullshit since they weren't that close.

CHAPTER 20

"Are we still going out on Friday night to Incahutes?" Peaches asked as she lay on her chest.

Chloe's hand was massaging her ass. "Didn't I say we was?" She replied.

They had just returned from the bar. Chloe was torn up from all the liquor that she drank, and so was Peaches. The liquor had both of them horny as ever. Peaches started kissing Chloe passionately, working her way down to her chest. Chloe closed her eyes and enjoyed the feeling of Peaches sucking on her nipples.

"Let me taste you," Peaches said while kissing her earlobes.

Peaches started sucking on her neck. Chloe felt the anticipation between her legs. She grew wet instantly and took a deep breath as she tried to control the wild sensations taking place within the folds of her pussy lips. Peaches got down on her knees, keeping her eyes on Chloe the entire time as she spread her legs apart. Chloe sucked in a sharp breath when she felt Peaches blowing on her pussy and placing two fingers deep inside of her moistness.

"Mmmmmm," Peaches moaned as she sucked on her fingers that had just been inside of Chloe. "I love it when you don't wear any panties."

She smiled at Chloe before pushing her legs even farther apart, making the dress she was wearing slide up her hips and out of the way. Peaches dove in without hesitation and without even thinking. Her tongue was making rings around Chloe's clit. *She has the best head game,* Chloe thought to herself.

Chloe had her share of men in her life, but no one could satisfy her like Peaches did. Actually, there was only one other person that could give Peaches a run for her money, and that was Lit.

Peaches slid her hand up under Chloe and grabbed onto her ass, pushing her forward so her pussy was at full display in front of her face. Peaches moaned, sucked, and licked her pussy lips as if she was eating her last meal. That feeling in Chloe's body was approaching for the third time in the last ten minutes, and she couldn't take any more. She kept trying to push Peaches away, but she wouldn't stop.

Peaches stuck her tongue deep inside Chloe's hole, and Chloe went crazy. Peaches's hair fell down over her face, and Chloe wrapped it around her hand and then pulled on it, making her tongue go deeper inside her now swollen walls. Chloe arched her back trying to meet each movement. The orgasm came so fast that it took her breath away. Peaches lifted up just enough to slip two fingers into her hole as she used her tongue to tickle her clit. That is when Chloe really exploded. Her juices poured out all in Peaches's mouth and over the sheets.

Chloe lay there completely exhausted. She pulled Peaches up and began kissing her. She returned the favor by pushing Peaches down and diving in headfirst. They went at it all night long, switching positions. Chloe fell asleep lying butt naked in the center of the bed.

Peaches got up and put on a robe. She walked out of the room and went downstairs. When she unlocked the door, two masked men rushed inside with guns in hand. They pushed Peaches out of the way and went straight upstairs as if they knew who they were looking for.

They walked into the room and saw Chloe's naked body sprawled out on the bed. Both of the men instantly bricked up at the sight before them. One of the masked men walked over and cocked his gun, aiming it at Chloe's head. He fired a shot and smiled at the hole he made. "I thought you weren't going to kill her," Peaches said, rushing into the room, but not seeing any blood.

"Shut up and get out of the way," the man said, wrapping Chloe's body up in a sheet. They lifted her up and carried her out of the house, placing her in the back of the SUV. "Are you coming or not?"

Peaches ran back into the house and put on her clothes. She grabbed her cell phone and car keys. She locked the door behind her and hopped in the backseat.

"When do I get my money?" She asked.

"Miss! You will get your money as soon as we get rid of your friend. You got some of it when we agreed to set this shit up, didn't you?" The driver asked.

Peaches shook her head and looked out the window as they drove through the park. She was nervous about what she had done and hoped that it didn't come back and bite her in the ass.

* * *

P-Funk and Derrick were standing on the sidewalk talking to Byron and Bricks. They were two young bulls that lived on the block. You could see in their eyes and tell that they were hungry to get in the game. Instead of diving in, P-Funk was trying to school them. He sparked up the pineapple games they had bought from the Mom and Pops on 25th. They passed them around as they watched Derrick serve the fiends that came on the block.

"Can I bring you back five dollars later for a bundle?" The girl said to Derrick, holding out the short money in her hand.

"You can come back when your money is straight. Don't nobody take shorts on this block," he replied.

"Please, I'll do anything. My body really needs this shit now," she said, with pleading eyes.

Derrick looked at the girl and couldn't believe she was strung out on dope. She was a beautiful, young Spanish girl. He had never seen her around there before. She had on a pair of tights, and he could see her pussy lips poking out in front. He looked over at P-Funk and told him he would be right back.

"Yo. Let me holla at you in the alley real quick," he said, walking toward the path between his crib. The girl followed him, already knowing what it was about. "Let me see what your head game is about."

"So you're going to give it to me for free if I do this?" she asked, licking her lips.

"If you got skills, I'll give you two," he stated, unzipping his pants, and pulling out his erect penis.

The girl looked around to make sure nobody was looking, got down on her knees and took his dick in her hands. She massaged his scrotum, tracing each ball with her fingertips. Derrick enjoyed the touch and sighed from the pleasure. She opened her mouth wide and bit down into his penis with immense force. She pressed down hard on his dick, grinding her teeth while shaking her head frantically from side to side like a predator devouring its prey. Derrick squealed like a slaughtered hog and fell to the ground in pain.

P-Funk, Bricks, and Byron heard the scream and looked over toward the sound. They walked over to the alley to see what was going on. When P-Funk looked down the alley, the girl was standing on top of Derrick looking down at him.

"What the fuck are you doing?" P-Funk shouted as he walked up on them.

The girl turned around and pointed a gun at him. Bricks and Byron quickly backed out of the alley, leaving P-Funk still standing there. She no longer looked like a smoker to them.

"Whoooaaa, ma! What is this all about?" P-Funk said, holding his hands up.

"Hit-Man sends his regards!" The girl said, aiming at Terrance and pulling the trigger.

Boca! Boca!

P-Funk tried to rush her, but she was quick on the draw. She turned and fired three shots at him. P-Funk fell face first on the ground. Knowing that someone heard the shots, the girl ran through the alley to the other side and jumped into the car waiting for her. They sped off down 18th.

Bricks and Byron had grabbed the guns that P-Funk stashed under the car tires, and they ran toward the screeching tires. They saw the car speeding down the streets and opened fire on it. People were sitting outside and began to take cover so they wouldn't get hit by a stray bullet. They missed their target but sent a warning to whomever it was not to come back. They ran back to Melon Street and hid the guns. They wanted to see what was going on with their old heads.

Cops were coming up the block, followed by fire and rescue. Bricks stood outside his aunt's door and watched the commotion going on. Derrick was dead, and they rushed P-Funk to the hospital. Detectives flooded the block, messing up everybody from getting money. Everything was shut down.

Bricks had P-Funk's trap phone and saw his brother's number on it. He called to inform him of what had just transpired and to tell him what hospital they took P-Funk to. Besides the phone, Bricks knew where P-Funk's work was at, so if somebody hit him up for something, he was going to help his big homie out and show him he was ready for the streets.

* * *

T-Baby got the news about P-Funk and was there twenty minutes later to check on his brother. He was in surgery, so he waited for the doctor to bring him the news. He kept trying to reach his other brother, but he didn't contact him, so he used Facebook and Instagram to reach him.

Three hours later, P-Funk was out of surgery. T-Baby was able to go to his room to visit. When he walked in, P-Funk looked at him and gave his little brother a slight smile, but T-Baby could sense something wasn't right.

"What's up, bro? How are you doing?" T-Baby said, walking over and standing next to him.

P-Funk lay in the hospital bed with a colonoscopy bag attached to his stomach. He stared at T-Baby for a second before responding.

"The bitch should have killed me. What the fuck am I supposed to do carrying around this fucking shit bag?"

"Who did this to you? When I finish with them, they will never forget the Freidlanders'," T-Baby stated, with venom in his eyes.

"I don't know who that bitch was," P-Funk replied.

While they were sitting there talking, a detective walked into the room. He carried a small file in one hand and his wallet with his credentials in the other. T-Baby and P-Funk knew who he was before he flashed his badge. They could smell a cop a mile away.

"Sorry to bug you, Keyonte," Detective Eli began, calling P-Funk by his government name. "I have to ask you some questions about what happened on the 1600 block Clay Street."

"We don't know anything, so you can turn around and walk the fuck back out the door," T-Baby barked at the cop.

"Listen, K! I know all about the both of you. I know what type of shit the Freidlander-Smith family is into, so miss me with that bullshit you talking. You already lost one brother to the streets. Do you want to lose another one?"

The detective was referring to their brother who everyone thought was dead but was living a whole new life in Florida. Only a few people knew he was alive and well. That's how he wanted it to be until he was able to walk the streets of Philly once again. He was actually going to change his facial identity as well.

P-Funk just sat there listening to his brother and the cop argue back and forth. If he wasn't in so much pain, he would have been involved too. He listened intently to what the detective was saying, as thoughts flashed through his mind.

"We have nothing to say to you, so can you roll out and let my brother rest," T-Baby barked, walking over to the door, and holding it open for Detective Eli to exit.

"Here's my card, just in case you want to talk," the detective said, dropping it on the table next to P-Funk's bed.

"Fucking pig," T-Baby said, closing the door behind him.

The two of them talked for about an hour before P-Funk's medication started kicking in. T-Baby stayed until he drifted off to sleep, and went out to get some answers on his own. From what his brother had told him, he didn't know what that shit was about. He wasn't trying to be on that type of time again, but when you fuck with family, the streets will mourn. Later that night, P-Funk needed to make a call that was important.

* * *

Derrick had his janaza at the mosque three days later. Being a Muslim, he had to be buried while the flesh was still warm. He was laid to rest at the cemetery in the southwest, right off of Indian

Creek. Four people got down into the grave as they passed them his body, which was wrapped in a white sheet. They laid him on his side and then climbed out. Everyone took turns with a shovel and placed dirt over the body to fill up the grave.

After they left the cemetery, everyone went back to Derrick's mom's house, where his sisters and aunts made all kinds of food. The house was so crowded that it looked like they were having a block party. It was starting to get dark, so the streetlights came on. Everyone gathered around to hold a memorial for Derrick for the last time of the night.

Derrick's sisters were talking to her cousin when her left eye kept jumping. She couldn't shake the feeling that something was about to go down. Her mom told her when she was little that if your left eye jumps, that means bad luck, and she could tell that a storm was brewing. She just didn't know what.

"What's wrong, cuz?" Vanda asked, sensing the change in her cousin's demeanor.

"I'm not sure yet, but something is about to go down."

"Girl, you are tripping. Come on, they are reminiscing about T."

The girls joined the circle to listen to all the people giving her brother compliments. Vanda stood next to P-Funk, who was out of the hospital now, and held his hand. The memorial went well, and after everybody started leaving, P-Funk, Vanda, and a couple of other people stayed outside, sitting around, talking, and drinking.

A van was driving through the block and stopped right in front of them. The side door opened, and four men jumped out menacingly with big guns drawn. They were all dressed in black and were ready to kill.

"Move and die," one man said, waving a machine gun around.

No one moved a muscle.

Vanda was petrified as the men walked up to P-Funk and one of them smacked him across the head with the butt of a gun. He almost fell out of the wheelchair, but two of the men caught him. They dragged him over to the van and threw him inside. They all got back in the van and pulled off. Vanda screamed and pulled out her cell phone, trying to take a picture of the license plate. But the van hit the corner before she could. She dialed 911 and told them what had just happened.

They patrolled the whole area, but there was no sign of the van anywhere. Vanda was so scared because her feeling had been right. Now, she hoped that P-Funk was still alive. Bricks had gone to record some music, so he didn't know what had happened until he came back on the block. There was nothing he could do, so he, along with everybody else, just waited to hear something.

CHAPTER 21

A lot of shit had been going down in the last couple of days. Muthafuckas were dropping off the face of the earth, and nobody knew what had happened. Xavier and Poncho had been putting in work for their boss, and the streets were now starting to see who was in charge. They were a two-man wrecking crew, but they had a team of niggas that Lit had put at their disposal, and they were straight killers with nothing to lose. Lit promised them that if anything happened to them, he would take care of their families.

"Yo, bro! This shit is like taking candy from a baby. We putting in work for big homie, and we don't even have to bust our gun right now," Xavier said.

"This shit ain't cool, dawg! I'm trying to put in some work and not sit around here while everybody is having fun," Poncho replied while taking a sip of Cîroc.

"We have plenty of time for that," Xavier said, taking the bottle from him and taking a sip. "Niggas' teams are weak out here right now, and pretty soon we will own everything."

"Don't you mean that nigga Lit will own everything? He's the money man right now. We working for him. It's not the other way around."

"For now."

"What you mean by that? That nigga is very well connected. I'm no sucka, but he can get us touched anywhere," Poncho stated, holding up his .40 caliber. "If you trying to take down his shit too, I'm with you."

Xavier knew his boy was a livewire, but he wasn't crazy enough to go at a cartel. They just got out of one beef with the Mexicans, and it would only be them. That was out of the question for now.

"Fuck all that. Let's go hit that last spot. The goons are in the car waiting for us. Load up, nigga," Xavier said.

They both gripped a couple of automatic weapons and headed out the door. They had found out there was a spot on Ponce where the niggas that shot at them, frequently hung out. It was time to pay them a visit.

When they pulled up to the crib, they could see people going in and out of the house. Xavier assumed it was a DJ house. He thought about just shooting it up and leaving, but he wanted what was inside.

"Y'all niggas ready?" he asked, cocking back the gun. "We taking everything they got and killing anything moving."

Everybody was locked and loaded, ready to move. Poncho was the first one out of the car, followed by Xavier and the rest of their soldiers. They were dressed in all black and wore ski masks. The soldiers surrounded the house with the efficiency of a SWAT team. One of the men knocked on the door, looking like he wanted some drugs. When it opened, Poncho stepped out first and fired three shots.

The first shot hit the man who opened the door in the throat and went straight through the back of his neck. The second and third shots hit him execution style in the head and heart. That's when all hell broke out. The people inside were ready for something like this. They didn't know how the intruders had gotten past the first wave of security, but they sure as hell weren't getting out of there alive.

Woody was upstairs talking to King on the phone about the new shipment of heroin being delivered in the morning when he heard the shots.

"What the fuck!" Woody yelled, looking at the monitor. "We're under attack, bro. I gotta go!"

"I'm on my way!" King said, hanging up and running into the bedroom of his house.

He lifted up his mattress and grabbed his .50 caliber handgun and one of his new toys that he just bought earlier, a Mak-90, that when fired sounded like an AK-47. He rushed out the door to get to his partner. He was only ten minutes away, but he hoped it wasn't ten minutes too late.

Woody picked up his SKS fully automatic assault rifle and headed toward the action. Two men were walking up the steps in his direction as he let the SK talk. The bullets cut through the men's bodies, knocking them back down the steps. A barrage of bullets started flying his way, forcing him to back off and fall back into his room.

Xavier and Poncho were shooting it out with four men in the kitchen. Bullets were ripping through the kitchen counter, refrigerator, cabinets, and everything else, but they weren't finding their targets. As soon as one of the men tried to run for the back door, Xavier hit him with precision in the head. The man fell through the window, dying instantly.

The other three came up to fire, but Poncho had already changed positions and had the drop on them. They couldn't even get a shot off because Poncho's MP5 canceled that option, laying down all three men.

Xavier and Poncho noticed the work on the table. When they walked over to where the drugs were bagged up, they started stuffing everything into trash bags.

"Find out where they have the money!" Poncho yelled to a couple of his men.

Before the guys could make a move, the basement door opened and about five more men came rushing out, taking shots at them. The men who Poncho had instructed to find the money were hit over ten times by the assault weapons. Xavier and Poncho started taking aim practice, knocking the men off one by one.

Woody was cornered upstairs in his room. He hit the floor just in time to miss the bullets flying through the door. He only had one chance to get out of there alive, and that was the window. As soon as he heard them reloading, he leaped up and jumped through the second-floor window. He hit the ground with a hard thump and rolled. The excruciating pain didn't stop him from getting out of the way of the flying bullets.

King pulled up on the scene in the middle of the gunfire. He hopped out and let his cannon roar. Men were dropping all over the place. Woody had made it around the front and was helping King kill the men who were outside. Inside, Xavier and Poncho were holding their own, being outflanked by Woody' s crew but killing all of them.

"The back door!" Poncho screamed as he headed for it.

Xavier got up and followed him out. When they got to the front of the house, Xavier spotted Woody and King and fired in their direction.

King and Woody took cover behind a car and returned fire. The four men were going at it until cop cars started appearing from every direction. All four men began firing at the cops, causing some of them to crash or pull back. King looked in the direction of Xavier and Poncho.

"Another place and time, niggas!" he said.

"No question," Xavier replied as the four men retreated in different directions while trying to elude the police.

Black SUVs came flying down the block in the direction of the cops. Men jumped out with crazy firepower and unloaded on the police officers. The police tried retaliating, but they were no match for the assault team. Cops were dropping like flies as the assault team made sure the men got away, before they jumped back into the cars and pulled off.

When Xavier was somewhere safe, he tossed his weapon down a drain and changed out of the all-black outfit he had on. Both he and Poncho had put clothes on under the black camouflage, just in case. They were prepared. Xavier made it to the crib of some shortie he was fucking and knocked on the door. When she answered, he walked in and sat down on the couch.

"I need to use your phone real quick. It's important," he said anxiously.

She didn't even ask questions because she knew he was a bad boy. She retrieved her phone from her purse and gave it to him. He dialed Poncho's phone to make sure he was straight. Poncho answered on the fourth ring.

"Who this?"

"It's me, nigga! Are you cool?" Xavier asked.

"Yeah. I'm straight, bro. Why you calling from another phone?"

"Mine's still in the car. I hope they don't find that shit, or they can link all that shit back to us."

"You should be alright, bro. What the fuck was that, though? Who were those muthafuckas who pulled up and popped off on the pigs?" Poncho asked.

"I don't know, but they had some big shit that I never seen before. I'm glad they were helping us," Xavier replied.

"I called big homie, and he wants us to meet with him first thing in the morning. People are calling for a truce because everybody is losing money right now, and they don't want to beef no more."

"That's 'cause they met their match. Pick me up in the morning. I'm going to kick it with my shortie tonight," Xavier said, looking over at the boy shorts and wifebeater his girl was wearing.

"Okay, be safe and knock that bitch back out, nigga," Poncho said jokingly.

"I got you, nigga," Xavier told him before hanging up.

CHAPTER 22

It had been a couple of days since the big massacre that took place in Ensley. More than ten cops had been killed in the line of duty, and the Mayor of Birmingham and the top brass were livid. They thought it was in retaliation for the shooting that had happened in Mobile. That was until they saw all the dead bodies sprawled inside and outside the house. The Mayor even asked the Governor for help, and to declare a state of emergency and call in the National Guard, but the Governor told him to hold off and let the feds handle it.

The real reason the Governor did that was because he was also in the cartel's pocket. He had talked to his employers and let them know there was a snitch in their organization. The mole had given up some valuable information, and the feds were planning to come down hard on them. But because of the cop killings, it was much worse. That was another reason a truce was called. They needed to find the mole and get rid of him.

Lit and Hit-Man were sitting in Lit's penthouse that he had bought to get away from Chester. He didn't want anybody trying to catch him slipping out there. Doja had been by his side, so he moved her and her daughter in with him. They were making too much money to stay in that place. There would be so many targets on their backs. The stickup boys were always lurking.

"No one can stop us now, bro. The competition is no longer a problem, and everybody knows that we run the city," Hit-Man stated, sipping on a glass of E&J.

Lit sat on the ottoman, puffing on some loud as he thought about all the treacherous things he and his crew had done to take over the city. They had committed so many murders to get that respect.

"Yeah, but where does that leave us now? We lost a lot of good soldiers in the process, and we don't know if it's truly over yet," Lit replied.

"Speaking of soldiers, we still haven't heard from Chloe yet, and she hasn't answered any of our calls."

"That is strange, but she and that girl are probably out enjoying that money and having some fun," Lit said, pouring himself another glass of liquor. "I'm hoping the streets haven't taken her too."

"Niggas always saying they are going to leave the game alone, but never do."

"Well, I'm going to show you better than I can tell you. I'm tired of all the drama and having to watch my back from those alphabet boys or niggas trying to be the man. I have two kids to raise, and they need me around, bro," Lit said.

"This is our life, man. This is all we know. For as the law or those niggas out here goes, they either get with the program or get deleted," he stated, with a sinister look on his face. "Anyway, what do you have in mind?"

"I was thinking about investing in a couple of things. First, look at what's going on in Atlantic City with the casinos. How about we look into that or maybe some apartment complex?" Lit asked.

"That sounds good and all, but how the hell are we going to get into that when neither of us has any business experience? We both dropped out of high school and have criminal records. How the hell we going to do that—"legally, that is?"

"I can get Doja to get a business license, and we have friends who can help with lenders. You let me worry about that part, and you worry about keeping our money flowing. Speaking of money, let's get out of here and go check on it. We'll let Xavier and Poncho relax today after all the shit they did. Besides, I have to pick up my kids and take them to Discovery Zone. I haven't spent time with them because of the beef."

The two men headed out of the penthouse to take care of their business. As they stepped off the elevator and headed toward the garage where their cars were parked, they never saw the three black SUVs creeping up on them, until it was too late.

The twelve men jumped out, aiming guns at Lit and Hit-Man. They wanted to reach for their weapons, but that would have the middle car smoking a Dutch.

"Gentlemen, my name is Darren. My employer would like to talk to the both of you."

"I'm not going anywhere. Tell him if he or she wants to speak to me, they can meet me on neutral ground," Hit-Man said, not backing down.

"It's not a request," Darren said.

Just then, both men felt a sting on the back of their necks. Before they had a chance to see who just had poked them, they fell to the ground. Lit's eyes started getting heavy, but not before he saw who was holding the needle in her hand. He passed out just as darkness claimed him.

* * *

Oh damn! My head hurts! Lit thought, trying to focus on where he was.

When his eyes adjusted to the little bit of light coming into the room, he could see he wasn't alone.

Lit tried to speak, but no words came out of his mouth. That's when he realized his mouth was gagged. He tried to move, but his hands and legs were also tied. He looked for Hit-Man and spotted him with his head down. There were at least four other people in the room with him, but he didn't recognize any of them.

Just then, the door opened, the lights came on, and about ten goons wearing masks entered the room. They were followed by two men, one of whom had grabbed him, and a woman. When Lit saw who the woman was, anger instantly flushed his body.

"I'm glad you're finally awake. Sorry for the in convenience, but precautions had to be taken for the good of everyone," Miguel said. "We are just waiting for the last person so we can get this party started."

Lit was trying to say something, but his sounds were muffled by the rag in his mouth. Miguel nodded, and Darren walked over to Lit and removed the gag.

"What the fuck is going on, Miguel? I thought we had an understanding? Why am I here, and what is she here for?" He said, pointing at Peaches. "You must want to go to war, so you might as well kill me now."

Mr. Wilmore, if I wanted to kill you, you would already be dead. I'm a respectable businessman, and I was asked to gather up all of you and hold you, by someone higher than me. However, you will get to know who this lady is very soon."

Lit's mind started racing as he thought about who would want him and Hit-Man. He was also wondering who the other three people were, whose heads were covered by pillowcases.

Miguel must have been reading his mind. He signaled over, and one of his men pulled the masks off of each one of the people. It was Chloe, P-Funk, and someone Lit never expected to see: Carlos.

If Carlos was a top boss, why the hell was he tied up in a chair? Lit had many questions that needed to be answered, and from what Miguel had said, the person to answer them was on his way. Was it Miguel? Why would he treat his partner like that, and what did he want with him? Why didn't he just call him over to his office? Question after question flooded through Lit's mind, and there was only one person who could answer them.

"Where is this person?"

"Be patient, my friend. He will be here in a minute, and all of your questions will be answered. Would you like a drink of water?" Miguel asked his prisoners.

No one responded.

Everyone was scared except for Lit and Chloe. She was wondering why she was there as well. One thing was for sure, if it was her time to go, she wasn't going out like a pussy.

Suddenly, the door opened, which caused everyone to look in that direction.

The man who everyone was waiting for walked in, and they all stood at attention. Miguel met him halfway to greet him.

"Gracias por venir. Quiero una bebida? (Thank you for coming. Want a drink?)" Miguel asked, shaking the man's hand.

"Estoy bien gracias (I am fine, thank you)," he replied.

Lit saw who it was, and he couldn't believe who was back in Philly. P-Funk also noticed who it was and knew that niggas was in trouble.

The man walked up to everyone who was tied to a chair and stared at them.

"Why are they tied up?" he asked, looking over at Miguel.

He was about to answer but thought twice about it when he saw the look on the man's face. "Untie them now!" Miguel barked.

Four goons rushed over to the captives and untied them.

"Follow me. I have prepared a meal. After you eat, we'll talk about why you are all here," the man told them.

Lit, Hit-Man, Chloe, P-Funk, and Carlos all followed the man into the other room, where there was a huge oval table covered with a tablecloth. There were ten plates of food and eleven chairs, but only seven people.

"Everyone sit down and eat," the man said. They all sat down and started eating.

"I brought you all here because we have a snake in our midst. Somebody here has been giving info to the wrong people, and a couple of my organizations in Florida have been raided, and they're working their way back here. So it's simple. I need to know which one of you has been running your fucking mouth."

"I hate snitches," Lit said, being the first to speak.

He looked dead at the man standing before him.

"We had a long talk before, and I said something to you. Did you listen to anything I said?"

Lit thought about what they talked about, and was about to respond, until four more people were escorted in at gunpoint. The man didn't even turn around.

"Have a seat and eat up."

It was Xavier, Poncho, King, and Woody They all took a seat and poured some wine in their glasses. The servers brought in meat and placed a piece on each plate.

"This smells good. What kind of meat is it?" Woody asked as he took a bite.

No one answered. They all started eating while they waited to hear who the snitch was.

Chloe already was anxious to know so she could put a bullet through their skull for putting her through this. She also wanted to know who this man was with all the power. He intrigued her.

"As you know, there is one empty seat. That's because he was responsible for hiring all of you, so it's his fault that we have a snitch in our presence," the man said.

"Where is he? I'll kill him for you and everybody else. I'll also body the nigga that's making it hot," Chloe said, standing up.

"That won't be necessary, lil lady. Miguel is not the problem anymore. Someone at this table is, though. To answer your question about Miguel's whereabouts—" the man paused before continuing "—you're eating him."

Everybody dropped their forks and started gagging. They couldn't believe what had just happened to them. Lit hoped like hell that he heard him wrong. When he didn't see any signs of a smile, he knew right then just how crazy this man was.

"Now that I have your attention, back to the matter at hand. Today, someone is going to die for deceiving me and this organization. See, the thing about having power is having everyone on the payroll. I had someone watching all of you, and you didn't even know it. Let me introduce you to the person who has been an agent for the FBI and told me about the mole in my organization. Send her in," he said to one of the guards.

A couple of minutes later, Peaches walked in and stood by the table. Chloe was more shocked than anybody because of the relationship she thought she had and all the things they did together, only to find out the whole time she was a fed.

"Don't look so shocked, Chloe. You know we will do whatever it takes to get the information we need," Peaches told her. "I played on your emotions, and it worked to my advantage."

"I should kill your ass!" Chloe stated, jumping up from the table.

Two huge guards immediately aimed their weapons at her.

"Everyone settle down. One of you will be dead by the end of tonight. For those of you who don't know her, I would like to introduce you to Agent Pryor. See, instead of her working with her counterparts, she has been working for me. What better spy than an actual agent. That way, I have tabs on both sides. She's the one who gave me the disturbing news."

"So, why do you have me sitting here like some fucking snitch?" Lit asked. "That's not in my bloodline."

"Because you had that snitch on your team, and it's because of you and your team that I had to destroy a large amount of my warehouses, among other things."

"Fuck am I here for then?" P-Funk said.

"Everyone, this is my big brother, right here!" The man said, walking over toward P-Funk. "I brought you here to take over the PA organization and to confront the muthafucka that had you touched."

At that moment, two guards grabbed Miguel and relieved him of his weapon. They passed the gun to P-Funk, who stood up, holding his stomach; and without saying a word, he emptied the clip into Miguel's body. The guards quickly moved out of the way as his body danced in place. He was dead before he hit the floor. P-Funk sat back down ice-grilling Hit-Man like he wanted to kill him too. He thought it was him that set him up.

The room was so quiet that one could hear a pin drop. Everyone was looking around wondering who would be next. Xavier was in deep thought about something, and then it finally hit him. "You're E.J.?"

"That is correct!" E.J. said, looking at Xavier. "I know everybody thought I was dead, but here I am in the flesh. It's amazing what money can buy for the right price."

Only a few people were around when he came to the building to see Lit. That's why there were so many shocked faces. E.J. didn't care who knew his identity now. When he found out that his brother got shot, he knew it was time to appear again, but this time to everyone.

"Now, back to the matter at hand. If there's one thing I hate more than a child molester, it's a snitch. So this is your one and only chance to get right with not only yourself but with God and confess your transgressions in front of the round table," E.J. said, removing his gun from the small of his back.

He then sat down at the head of the table and waited.

Everyone looked around the table at each other, but no one said anything. They were all suspicious of the next person, wondering who the snitch was.

"You have sixty seconds to admit your guilt. God forgives, but I don't. Deceit is punishable by death in my eyes. I don't care who you are."

That minute seemed like it went by in fifteen seconds. E.J. stood up gripping his gun in his right hand. He walked over to the ninety-inch big screen television hanging on the wall and turned it on. One of his men passed him a flash drive, which he plugged it in.

"I'm about to show you who the person is that was infiltrating my organization. I would have spared you, but you wouldn't confess, and now it's too late," E.J. said, pressing the power button to the television.

When the photo of the snitch appeared on the screen, everyone in the room gasped. It showed a group of people sitting around a desk talking to a shadow. One of E.J.' s men walked over and took the gun that P-Funk was holding. He passed it to E.J. and stepped back, because he already knew what was about to happen.

Lit was shocked and looked over at the screen to make sure he was seeing correctly. The screen wouldn't reveal the face of the person because it was blurred out. They all remembered having a meeting like that before, so it could be any of them.

"Let's just get this over with so we can get back to business," E.J. announced.

He removed the clip from the gun, replacing it with a fresh one. His men all cocked their weapons and aimed at the table. E.J. started walking around the table, pointing the gun toward the back of each person's head.

"Sorry, but this is just business, and you picked the wrong fucking ones," he said, stopping and blowing off the back of the snitch's head. Blood splattered everywhere, getting all over them.

"Now, let's get back to work."

E.J. walked out of the room, never looking back at the carnage he had just left.

To Be Continued…
Real G's Move in Silence 2
Coming Soon

Lock Down Publications and Ca$h Presents assisted publishing packages.

BASIC PACKAGE $499
Editing
Cover Design
Formatting

UPGRADED PACKAGE $800
Typing
Editing
Cover Design
Formatting

ADVANCE PACKAGE $1,200
Typing
Editing
Cover Design
Formatting
Copyright registration
Proofreading
Upload book to Amazon

LDP SUPREME PACKAGE $1,500
Typing
Editing
Cover Design
Formatting
Copyright registration
Proofreading
Set up Amazon account
Upload book to Amazon
Advertise on LDP Amazon and Facebook page

***Other services available upon request. Additional charges may apply

Lock Down Publications
P.O. Box 944
Stockbridge, GA 30281-9998
Phone # 470 303-9761

Submission Guideline

Submit the first three chapters of your completed manuscript to ldpsubmissions@gmail.com, subject line: Your book's title. The manuscript must be in a .doc file and sent as an attachment. Document should be in Times New Roman, double spaced and in size 12 font. Also, provide your synopsis and full contact information. If sending multiple submissions, they must each be in a separate email.

Have a story but no way to send it electronically? You can still submit to LDP/Ca$h Presents. Send in the first three chapters, written or typed, of your completed manuscript to:

LDP: Submissions Dept
Po Box 944
Stockbridge, Ga 30281

DO NOT send original manuscript. Must be a duplicate.

Provide your synopsis and a cover letter containing your full contact information.

Thanks for considering LDP and Ca$h Presents.

NEW RELEASES

THE BRICK MAN 5 by KING RIO

BABY I'M WINTERTIME COLD 2 by MEESHA

MONEY MAFIA 2 by JIBRIL WILLIAMS

REAL G'S MOVE IN SILENCE by VON DIESEL

Coming Soon from Lock Down Publications/Ca$h Presents

BLOOD OF A BOSS **VI**

SHADOWS OF THE GAME II

TRAP BASTARD II

By **Askari**

LOYAL TO THE GAME **IV**

By **T.J. & Jelissa**

TRUE SAVAGE **VIII**

MIDNIGHT CARTEL IV

DOPE BOY MAGIC IV

CITY OF KINGZ III

NIGHTMARE ON SILENT AVE II

THE PLUG OF LIL MEXICO II

CLASSIC CITY II

By **Chris Green**

BLAST FOR ME **III**

A SAVAGE DOPEBOY III

CUTTHROAT MAFIA III

DUFFLE BAG CARTEL VII

HEARTLESS GOON VI

By **Ghost**

A HUSTLER'S DECEIT III

KILL ZONE II

BAE BELONGS TO ME III

TIL DEATH II

By **Aryanna**

KING OF THE TRAP III

By **T.J. Edwards**

GORILLAZ IN THE BAY V

3X KRAZY III

STRAIGHT BEAST MODE III

De'Kari

KINGPIN KILLAZ IV

STREET KINGS III

PAID IN BLOOD III

CARTEL KILLAZ IV

DOPE GODS III

Hood Rich

SINS OF A HUSTLA II

ASAD

YAYO V

Bred In The Game 2

S. Allen

THE STREETS WILL TALK II

By Yolanda Moore

SON OF A DOPE FIEND III

HEAVEN GOT A GHETTO II

SKI MASK MONEY II

By Renta

LOYALTY AIN'T PROMISED III

By Keith Williams

I'M NOTHING WITHOUT HIS LOVE II

SINS OF A THUG II

TO THE THUG I LOVED BEFORE II

IN A HUSTLER I TRUST II

By Monet Dragun

QUIET MONEY IV

EXTENDED CLIP III

THUG LIFE IV

By **Trai'Quan**

THE STREETS MADE ME IV

By **Larry D. Wright**

IF YOU CROSS ME ONCE II

ANGEL V

By **Anthony Fields**

THE STREETS WILL NEVER CLOSE IV

By K'ajji

HARD AND RUTHLESS III

KILLA KOUNTY IV

By Khufu

MONEY GAME III

By Smoove Dolla

JACK BOYS VS DOPE BOYS IV

A GANGSTA'S QUR'AN V

COKE GIRLZ II

COKE BOYS II

LIFE OF A SAVAGE V

CHI'RAQ GANGSTAS V

By Romell Tukes

MURDA WAS THE CASE III

Elijah R. Freeman

THE STREETS NEVER LET GO III

By Robert Baptiste

AN UNFORESEEN LOVE IV

BABY, I'M WINTERTIME COLD III

By **Meesha**

QUEEN OF THE ZOO III

By **Black Migo**

VICIOUS LOYALTY III

By Kingpen

A GANGSTA'S PAIN III

By J-Blunt

CONFESSIONS OF A JACKBOY III

By Nicholas Lock

GRIMEY WAYS III

By Ray Vinci

KING KILLA II

By Vincent "Vitto" Holloway

BETRAYAL OF A THUG III

By Fre$h

THE MURDER QUEENS III

By Michael Gallon

THE BIRTH OF A GANGSTER III

By Delmont Player

TREAL LOVE II

By Le'Monica Jackson

FOR THE LOVE OF BLOOD III

By Jamel Mitchell

RAN OFF ON DA PLUG II

By Paper Boi Rari

HOOD CONSIGLIERE III

By Keese

PRETTY GIRLS DO NASTY THINGS II

By Nicole Goosby

PROTÉGÉ OF A LEGEND II

By Corey Robinson

IT'S JUST ME AND YOU II

By Ah'Million

BORN IN THE GRAVE III

By Self Made Tay

FOREVER GANGSTA III

By Adrian Dulan

GORILLAZ IN THE TRENCHES II

By SayNoMore

THE COCAINE PRINCESS VI

By King Rio

CRIME BOSS II

Playa Ray

LOYALTY IS EVERYTHING II

Molotti

HERE TODAY GONE TOMORROW II

By Fly Rock

REAL G'S MOVE IN SILENCE II

By Von Diesel

Available Now

RESTRAINING ORDER **I & II**

By **CA$H & Coffee**

LOVE KNOWS NO BOUNDARIES **I II & III**

By **Coffee**

RAISED AS A GOON I, II, III & IV

BRED BY THE SLUMS I, II, III

BLAST FOR ME I & II

ROTTEN TO THE CORE I II III

A BRONX TALE I, II, III

DUFFLE BAG CARTEL I II III IV V VI

HEARTLESS GOON I II III IV V

A SAVAGE DOPEBOY I II

DRUG LORDS I II III

CUTTHROAT MAFIA I II

KING OF THE TRENCHES

By **Ghost**

LAY IT DOWN **I & II**

LAST OF A DYING BREED I II

BLOOD STAINS OF A SHOTTA I & II III

By **Jamaica**

LOYAL TO THE GAME I II III

LIFE OF SIN I, II III

By **TJ & Jelissa**

BLOODY COMMAS I & II

SKI MASK CARTEL I II & III

KING OF NEW YORK I II,III IV V

RISE TO POWER I II III

COKE KINGS I II III IV V

BORN HEARTLESS I II III IV

KING OF THE TRAP I II

By **T.J. Edwards**

IF LOVING HIM IS WRONG…I & II

LOVE ME EVEN WHEN IT HURTS I II III

By **Jelissa**

WHEN THE STREETS CLAP BACK I & II III

THE HEART OF A SAVAGE I II III IV

MONEY MAFIA I II

LOYAL TO THE SOIL I II III

By **Jibril Williams**

A DISTINGUISHED THUG STOLE MY HEART I II & III

LOVE SHOULDN'T HURT I II III IV

RENEGADE BOYS I II III IV

PAID IN KARMA I II III

SAVAGE STORMS I II III

AN UNFORESEEN LOVE I II III

BABY, I'M WINTERTIME COLD I II

By **Meesha**

A GANGSTER'S CODE I &, II III

A GANGSTER'S SYN I II III

THE SAVAGE LIFE I II III

CHAINED TO THE STREETS I II III

BLOOD ON THE MONEY I II III

A GANGSTA'S PAIN I II

By J-Blunt

PUSH IT TO THE LIMIT

By **Bre' Hayes**

BLOOD OF A BOSS **I, II, III, IV, V**

SHADOWS OF THE GAME

TRAP BASTARD

By **Askari**

THE STREETS BLEED MURDER **I, II & III**

THE HEART OF A GANGSTA I II& III

By **Jerry Jackson**

CUM FOR ME I II III IV V VI VII VIII

An **LDP Erotica Collaboration**

BRIDE OF A HUSTLA **I II & II**

THE FETTI GIRLS **I, II& III**

CORRUPTED BY A GANGSTA I, II III, IV

BLINDED BY HIS LOVE

THE PRICE YOU PAY FOR LOVE I, II ,III

DOPE GIRL MAGIC I II III

By **Destiny Skai**

WHEN A GOOD GIRL GOES BAD

By **Adrienne**

THE COST OF LOYALTY I II III

By Kweli

A GANGSTER'S REVENGE **I II III & IV**

THE BOSS MAN'S DAUGHTERS I II III IV V

A SAVAGE LOVE **I & II**

BAE BELONGS TO ME I II

A HUSTLER'S DECEIT I, II, III

WHAT BAD BITCHES DO I, II, III

SOUL OF A MONSTER I II III

KILL ZONE

A DOPE BOY'S QUEEN I II III

TIL DEATH

By **Aryanna**

A KINGPIN'S AMBITON

A KINGPIN'S AMBITION **II**

I MURDER FOR THE DOUGH

By **Ambitious**

TRUE SAVAGE I II III IV V VI VII

DOPE BOY MAGIC I, II, III

MIDNIGHT CARTEL I II III

CITY OF KINGZ I II

NIGHTMARE ON SILENT AVE

THE PLUG OF LIL MEXICO II

CLASSIC CITY

By **Chris Green**

A DOPEBOY'S PRAYER

By **Eddie "Wolf" Lee**

THE KING CARTEL **I, II & III**

By **Frank Gresham**

THESE NIGGAS AIN'T LOYAL **I, II & III**

By **Nikki Tee**

GANGSTA SHYT **I II &III**

By **CATO**

THE ULTIMATE BETRAYAL

By **Phoenix**

BOSS'N UP **I , II & III**

By **Royal Nicole**

I LOVE YOU TO DEATH

By **Destiny J**

I RIDE FOR MY HITTA

I STILL RIDE FOR MY HITTA

By **Misty Holt**

LOVE & CHASIN' PAPER

By **Qay Crockett**

TO DIE IN VAIN

SINS OF A HUSTLA

By **ASAD**

BROOKLYN HUSTLAZ

By **Boogsy Morina**

BROOKLYN ON LOCK I & II

By **Sonovia**

GANGSTA CITY

By **Teddy Duke**

A DRUG KING AND HIS DIAMOND I & II III

A DOPEMAN'S RICHES

HER MAN, MINE'S TOO I, II

CASH MONEY HO'S

THE WIFEY I USED TO BE I II

PRETTY GIRLS DO NASTY THINGS

By Nicole Goosby

TRAPHOUSE KING **I II & III**

KINGPIN KILLAZ I II III

STREET KINGS I II

PAID IN BLOOD **I II**

CARTEL KILLAZ I II III

DOPE GODS I II

By **Hood Rich**

LIPSTICK KILLAH **I, II, III**

CRIME OF PASSION I II & III

FRIEND OR FOE I II III

By **Mimi**

STEADY MOBBN' **I, II, III**

THE STREETS STAINED MY SOUL I II III

By **Marcellus Allen**

WHO SHOT YA **I, II, III**

SON OF A DOPE FIEND I II

HEAVEN GOT A GHETTO

SKI MASK MONEY

Renta

GORILLAZ IN THE BAY **I II III IV**

TEARS OF A GANGSTA I II

3X KRAZY I II

STRAIGHT BEAST MODE I II

DE'KARI

TRIGGADALE I II III

MURDAROBER WAS THE CASE I II

Elijah R. Freeman

GOD BLESS THE TRAPPERS I, II, III

THESE SCANDALOUS STREETS I, II, III

FEAR MY GANGSTA I, II, III IV, V

THESE STREETS DON'T LOVE NOBODY I, II

BURY ME A G I, II, III, IV, V

A GANGSTA'S EMPIRE I, II, III, IV

THE DOPEMAN'S BODYGAURD I II

THE REALEST KILLAZ I II III

THE LAST OF THE OGS I II III

Tranay Adams

THE STREETS ARE CALLING

Duquie Wilson

MARRIED TO A BOSS I II III

By Destiny Skai & Chris Green

KINGZ OF THE GAME I II III IV V VI

CRIME BOSS

Playa Ray

SLAUGHTER GANG I II III

RUTHLESS HEART I II III

By Willie Slaughter

FUK SHYT

By Blakk Diamond

DON'T F#CK WITH MY HEART I II

By Linnea

ADDICTED TO THE DRAMA I II III

IN THE ARM OF HIS BOSS II

By Jamila

YAYO I II III IV

A SHOOTER'S AMBITION I II

BRED IN THE GAME

By S. Allen

TRAP GOD I II III

RICH $AVAGE I II III

MONEY IN THE GRAVE I II III

By Martell Troublesome Bolden

FOREVER GANGSTA I II

GLOCKS ON SATIN SHEETS I II

By Adrian Dulan

TOE TAGZ I II III IV

LEVELS TO THIS SHYT I II

IT'S JUST ME AND YOU

By Ah'Million

KINGPIN DREAMS I II III

RAN OFF ON DA PLUG

By Paper Boi Rari

CONFESSIONS OF A GANGSTA I II III IV

CONFESSIONS OF A JACKBOY I II

By Nicholas Lock

I'M NOTHING WITHOUT HIS LOVE

SINS OF A THUG

TO THE THUG I LOVED BEFORE

A GANGSTA SAVED XMAS

IN A HUSTLER I TRUST

By Monet Dragun

CAUGHT UP IN THE LIFE I II III

THE STREETS NEVER LET GO I II

By Robert Baptiste

NEW TO THE GAME I II III

MONEY, MURDER & MEMORIES I II III

By **Malik D. Rice**

LIFE OF A SAVAGE I II III IV

A GANGSTA'S QUR'AN I II III IV

MURDA SEASON I II III

GANGLAND CARTEL I II III

CHI'RAQ GANGSTAS I II III IV

KILLERS ON ELM STREET I II III

JACK BOYZ N DA BRONX I II III

A DOPEBOY'S DREAM I II III

JACK BOYS VS DOPE BOYS I II III

COKE GIRLZ

COKE BOYS

By Romell Tukes

LOYALTY AIN'T PROMISED I II

By Keith Williams

QUIET MONEY I II III

THUG LIFE I II III

EXTENDED CLIP I II

A GANGSTA'S PARADISE

By **Trai'Quan**

THE STREETS MADE ME I II III

By **Larry D. Wright**

THE ULTIMATE SACRIFICE I, II, III, IV, V, VI

KHADIFI

IF YOU CROSS ME ONCE

ANGEL I II III IV

IN THE BLINK OF AN EYE

By **Anthony Fields**

THE LIFE OF A HOOD STAR

By Ca$h & Rashia Wilson

THE STREETS WILL NEVER CLOSE I II III

By K'ajji

CREAM I II III

THE STREETS WILL TALK

By Yolanda Moore

NIGHTMARES OF A HUSTLA I II III

By King Dream

CONCRETE KILLA I II III

VICIOUS LOYALTY I II

By Kingpen

HARD AND RUTHLESS I II

MOB TOWN 251

THE BILLIONAIRE BENTLEYS I II III

REAL G'S MOVE IN SILENCE

By Von Diesel

GHOST MOB

Stilloan Robinson

MOB TIES I II III IV V VI

SOUL OF A HUSTLER, HEART OF A KILLER

GORILLAZ IN THE TRENCHES

By SayNoMore

BODYMORE MURDERLAND I II III

THE BIRTH OF A GANGSTER I II

By Delmont Player

FOR THE LOVE OF A BOSS

By C. D. Blue

MOBBED UP I II III IV

THE BRICK MAN I II III IV V

THE COCAINE PRINCESS I II III IV V

By King Rio

KILLA KOUNTY I II III IV

By Khufu

MONEY GAME I II

By Smoove Dolla

A GANGSTA'S KARMA I II III

By FLAME

KING OF THE TRENCHES I II III

by **GHOST & TRANAY ADAMS**

QUEEN OF THE ZOO I II

By **Black Migo**

GRIMEY WAYS I II

By Ray Vinci

XMAS WITH AN ATL SHOOTER

By Ca$h & Destiny Skai

KING KILLA

By Vincent "Vitto" Holloway

BETRAYAL OF A THUG I II

By Fre$h

THE MURDER QUEENS I II

By Michael Gallon

TREAL LOVE

By Le'Monica Jackson

FOR THE LOVE OF BLOOD I II

By Jamel Mitchell

HOOD CONSIGLIERE I II

By Keese

PROTÉGÉ OF A LEGEND

By Corey Robinson

BORN IN THE GRAVE I II

By Self Made Tay

MOAN IN MY MOUTH

By XTASY

TORN BETWEEN A GANGSTER AND A GENTLEMAN

By J-BLUNT & Miss Kim

LOYALTY IS EVERYTHING

Molotti

HERE TODAY GONE TOMORROW

By Fly Rock

BOOKS BY LDP'S CEO, CA$H

TRUST IN NO MAN

TRUST IN NO MAN 2

TRUST IN NO MAN 3

BONDED BY BLOOD

SHORTY GOT A THUG

THUGS CRY

THUGS CRY 2

THUGS CRY 3

TRUST NO BITCH

TRUST NO BITCH 2

TRUST NO BITCH 3

TIL MY CASKET DROPS

RESTRAINING ORDER

RESTRAINING ORDER 2

IN LOVE WITH A CONVICT

LIFE OF A HOOD STAR

XMAS WITH AN ATL SHOOTER